W9-ABX-200

MURDER TAKES A BREAK

Other Walker Mysteries by Bill Crider

MURDER
TAKES
A
BREAK

A Truman Smith Mystery

BILL CRIDER 1941-

WALKER AND COMPANY
NEW YORK

First published in the United States of America in 1997 by
Walker Publishing Company, Inc.

Published simultaneously in Canada by Thomas Allen & Son Canada, Limited,
Markham, Ontario

Library of Congress Cataloging-in-Publication Data
Crider, Bill, 1941–
Murder takes a break: a Truman Smith novel/Bill Crider.
p. cm.
ISBN 0-8027-3308-5
1. Smith, Truman (Fictitious character)—Fiction. I. Title.
PS3553.R497M88   1997
813′.54—dc21   97-19939
                                             CIP

Printed in the United States of America
2 4 6 8 10 9 7 5 3 1

To Ed Gorman and Marty Greenberg

1

RANDALL KIRBO HAD come to Galveston in March for spring break. That had been nine months ago, and no one in his family had seen him since. As far as they knew, no one else had seen him, either. And now they wanted me to find him.

I didn't want to take the job. I used to do things like that for a living, but that was before my own sister had disappeared. You could say I'd found her, in a sense, but it had been far too late to do her any good.

And then there was the time I'd tried to find Dino's daughter. I'd found her, all right, but the less said about all that had happened then, the better, at least as far as I was concerned.

After that little bit of unpleasantness, I'd sort of given up my profession.

Dino thought it was time for me to take it up again. It wasn't the first time he'd asked.

"It's like a personal favor, Tru," he said. "You know I hate to ask you, but there it is."

He didn't hate to ask me at all, but he probably felt he had to say so.

"Let's see," I said. "The last time you asked me to do something, you said there was nothing to it. Just an old high school friend of ours who needed a little investigation done. But it didn't work out quite that way, did it?"

"Hey," Dino said, "that wasn't my fault. I thought it was just about some dead bird."

"Prairie chicken," I told him.

"Whatever. A bird's a bird, right?"

"Wrong," I said, but I didn't elaborate. I didn't figure that Dino wanted to hear a lecture on an endangered species. "And you were wrong about the job, too. I wound up getting shot at and beat up and—"

Dino raised a hand to stop me. "OK, OK, you win. It was a mistake for you to get involved. But it'll be different this time."

He stopped and waited for me to say something. So I said, "You forgot to say 'Trust me.'"

"Trust me," he said, with what might have been an honest attempt to look sincere.

"I feel a lot better already," I told him. "You want something to drink?"

We were in the living room of my house, which actually belonged to Dino. He was just letting me live there. I was sitting on my couch, which had been a really nice one in about 1956. Dino was in a chair that might have been a little newer, but not much. I got most of my furniture at garage sales.

"Not Big Red," Dino said. "Somebody told me that if you spill that stuff on a carpet, you can never get the stains out. No matter what you use."

Big Red was what I drank, and Dino was convinced that it was going to eat through my stomach lining any day now. He didn't much like the way it tasted, either, and now he was glancing around to see if there were any suspicious stains on the furniture. There were plenty, but it would be hard to say exactly what had caused them.

"I don't usually have guests," I told him. "So Big Red's about all I have on hand."

"You got any ginger ale?"

"You drank the last of it."

"That was months ago."

"Well, if you'd come out more often, I'd keep a bigger supply."

Dino didn't push it. His uncles had practically been the barons of Galveston Island years before, back in the days when you could go out on the long pier to the Island Retreat and drop your silver in their slot machines, watch the little clickety balls bounce around their roulette wheels, or lose as much as you could stand at blackjack.

But hurricanes had shortened the pier, the Texas Rangers had dumped the slots into the bay, the Island Retreat was closed, and Dino wasn't like his uncles. He preferred to stay in his house, which didn't even have a view of the water, and watch infomercials on TV.

"I don't get out much," he said. He was a master of understatement. "But I'm getting better at it."

That was true. He'd gotten together with Evelyn Matthews, the mother of his daughter, after a lapse of a lot of years, and she'd done wonders for him. He wasn't going to win the Outdoorsman of the Year award, but he wasn't spending all his waking minutes inside anymore. Most of them, yes, but not all.

"How about some water?" I asked.

"Water would be OK." He looked around the room. "Where's Nameless?"

Nameless was my cat. Or the cat who lived with me. You couldn't really say he was mine. He didn't belong to anybody other than himself.

"He's outside," I said. "Did you think he'd come to welcome you?"

Dino looked hurt. "I think he's beginning to like me."

"Maybe," I said, but I didn't think so.

For that matter, I didn't think Nameless really liked anybody. He liked chasing the little geckos that lived in the oleander bushes surrounding the house, and he liked having his head rubbed now and then. And eating. He liked eating more than just about anything. But I wasn't sure he had ever developed a real attachment to anyone human, even to me, and I was the one who provided his food.

I got off the couch and went into the kitchen to get the water. I decided I'd have water, too. Maybe Dino was right about my stomach lining. I took a plastic ice cube tray out of the refrigerator's freezer compartment and twisted it until the ice loosened up. Then I put four or five cubes in two glasses and filled them from the tap.

"Tastes great," Dino said when I gave him his glass and he'd taken a swallow.

"It's just water."

"Yeah." He took another drink. "But it's good water."

I looked at him. "You going to talk about how great the water is, or are you going to tell me some more about this personal favor you want me to do?"

He put his glass on the low wooden coffee table. The glass was beaded with moisture, and it would probably leave a ring, but that would be all right. There were plenty of other rings there to keep it company.

"You still look for people, right?"

"No. I don't look for people. You know that."

"Well, what you do is practically the same thing."

"No, it's not."

What I did now was all done right there in the house, with a computer. I did background checks, mostly. It's easy, and it's profitable. I run a little ad in the classified section of the Houston *Chronicle*, and I get plenty of calls from women who want to find out about the men they're dating, from businessmen who're considering hiring someone but aren't quite sure about the resumé they've been given, and from fathers who wonder about the guys who've been seeing their daughters.

If you ever sent in one of the little warranty cards that came with your new toaster or your new hair dryer, you're in a database somewhere, and I can find you.

Or if you've played around on the Internet and ordered one of those free CD-ROMs that car companies and state governments offer you, you've probably provided all kinds of information that I can get to.

If you have a telephone with a listed number, I can get your address in a few seconds.

Credit checks are just as simple if you know what you're doing, and I do. I worked for a bail bondsman for a while, and I learned a few tricks. I can even find out where you've used your credit card or an ATM.

If you're trying to hide something, it might take me a little longer to find out about you, but eventually I'll get there. Not everyone knows it, but thanks to the information superhighway, personal privacy is pretty much a thing of the past.

But checking on people the way I do is nothing like going out and actually looking for someone no one else can find, and Dino knows it. He also knows very well why I don't like doing it the hard way anymore.

"OK," he admitted. "It's not the same thing. But it's close. And like I said, this would be a personal favor."

"For you, or for someone else?"

"For me."

"But you're asking for someone else."

"Right."

"Why?"

"Well, see, Tack Kirbo's sort of an old friend."

"What kind of friend?"

"From college. I guess you don't remember him. He and I played football together."

I felt a twinge, but I didn't say anything. Dino knew what I was thinking, though.

"The knee doing OK these days?" he asked.

Dino had practically destroyed my knee with his helmet when he'd tackled me just as I was about to break away for a long run. On a beautiful fall day, he'd ended what most sportswriters thought was a great football career that was going to become even greater when I turned pro.

What had happened hadn't been Dino's fault, but he couldn't quite get over the idea that it had been.

"The knee's fine," I lied. "But I don't remember Kirbo. What position did he play?"

"He was mostly a backup. Played tight end. No reason you'd remember him."

"But you do."

"Sure. We were pretty good buddies in those days."

"And now he's lost his kid."

"Right. And the cops can't find him. No one can find him. I thought you might give it a try."

"As a personal favor. Sort of like when I looked for Outside Harry."

Outside Harry was a local character Dino had developed an attachment to. He'd disappeared not so long ago, and Dino had asked me to find him. I did, but not before nearly getting killed three or four times.

"That was different," Dino said. "You knew that might be dangerous."

"Sure I did."

"Tack would pay you, if that's what you're worried about."

"I'm not talking about money."

"You can be a real bastard sometimes, Tru."

I smiled. "You're only saying that because you like me."

"Fat chance. Will you do it or not?"

I thought about it. The people were missing their son, and while I didn't think I could help them, it wouldn't do any harm to talk to them. Or that's what I thought at the time.

"I'll talk to the Kirbos," I said. "As a personal favor."

Dino smiled. "I'd appreciate it," he said.

YOU CAN NEVER be sure what kind of weather to expect on Galveston Island in the winter. In 1886, so the story goes, the temperature dropped to somewhere near zero, and the bay froze to a depth of two and a half inches.

The day Dino drove me to see Tack Kirbo was different. According to the television news I'd seen a day or so earlier, it was snowing in New England and in upstate New York. In Seattle, there was a cold, drenching rain. The Midwest was freezing, and ice covered the highways.

But in Galveston, it was a lot like springtime, seventy degrees, a deep blue sky with not a cloud in sight, and a strong southerly breeze that whipped the gray-green Gulf of Mexico into second-rate whitecaps.

Gulls swooped and dipped over the waves as if some kid were pulling them on kite strings. Out near the horizon, oil rigs squatted over the water, and a tanker seemed painted on the sky.

I lived on the west end of the Island, and Dino hadn't wanted to drive along the seawall, but I'd insisted. Since he preferred to stay in his house, if he had to get out of it, he wanted to stay as far from the water as possible. But the Kirbos were staying in the Galvez Hotel, which is right on Seawall Boulevard. There was no use in going out of our way to avoid seeing the Gulf.

A girl in a skimpy halter top and tight cutoffs was skimming along the top of the wall on a pair of in-line skates. She had long legs, a blond ponytail that hung out from under her safety helmet, and skin the color of almonds.

"Aren't you glad you came this way?" I said.

Dino didn't answer. He looked straight ahead, as if he were having to concentrate on the traffic. There were only about four cars in sight.

"Want to stop and walk along one of the jetties?" I asked. "Have a look at the mural?"

The Gulf side of the seawall had been painted with what the tourist office was calling the world's longest mural, between Twenty-fifth and Sixty-first streets: surfers, giant clams, fish, waves—all kinds of briny stuff like that.

Dino cut his eyes in my direction. "You're kidding me," he said.

"It might do you good. You could get a little sun."

"Sun gives you skin cancer. I don't need that."

I thought about the girl on the skates. Dino was right, and I hated to think what might happen to her in twenty or thirty years. On the other hand, Dino looked like a man who'd just returned to the free world after doing twenty years in solitary in one of the fine units of the Texas Department of Criminal Justice. The Pillsbury Doughboy had as much color as he did. There had to be a reasonable compromise somewhere.

"How about that beach?" I said.

Dino didn't look. "It's not as big as it used to be," he said.

He was right about that, too, though the city had invested millions in widening the beachfront. The sand had been dredged off the bottom of the Gulf and pumped along the shoreline. The sand had smelled like the bilge in a shrimp boat for a while, but before long the smell had gone away and the beach had been almost as wide as I remembered it from my childhood, before storms and tides had carried most of the sand out into the Gulf. But after only a couple of years the beach had begun shrinking again. Nothing stays the same.

Nothing, that is, except for the Galvez Hotel, all two hundred and fifty rooms of it. It's been sitting right there behind the seawall, just across the street from the beach, since 1911. There are some people who think the hotel is even older than that, that it survived the big storm of 1900, but it didn't. In fact, one of the reasons it was built was to help Galveston recover from the devastating economic effects of that storm.

It did survive the hurricane that roared out of the Gulf in 1915, however. That storm wasn't nearly as bad as the one fifteen years earlier, but it was bad enough to tear four-ton granite boulders out of the jetties and toss them over the seawall while dancers in the Galvez's ballroom swirled and turned as if they didn't have a care in the world.

The Galvez is a huge white building, a lot like one of those resort hotels you see on old picture postcards, with palm trees and couples dressed all in white playing croquet on wide expanses of lawn. Lots of famous people have stayed there. Phil Harris and Alice Faye—remember them?—were married there, a long time ago.

The Galvez doesn't have much of a lawn, but there are palm trees, all right, except that today the trunks of the palm trees in front of the hotel were ringed from bottom to top with white Christmas lights. Christmas lights on palm trees had always struck me as pretty strange, but, as far as I could tell, it didn't appear to bother anyone else. Certainly not Dino, who didn't even seem to notice. He turned his big old Pontiac off Seawall Boulevard and pulled around to the back of the hotel to enter the parking lot.

He locked the car when we got out, and we walked past a BFI Dumpster to the back entrance. There were several chartered buses parked along the walk.

"Dickens on the Strand," Dino said.

I'd forgotten about that. Every year, one weekend early in December, there's a pseudo-Victorian Christmas celebration along the Strand, an area of restored buildings and shops near the docks. I've never participated in the festivities, and I was willing to bet that Dino hadn't, either. Plenty of tourists showed up for the fun, however, as the chartered buses, from San Antonio, Waco, and Dallas, proved.

We went through the doors and up the steps into the lobby, where there was a fifteen-foot-tall Christmas tree, decorated with gold ribbons and red balls. To our right were the elevators and the check-in desk, and on our left handbells of all sizes lay on top of a long table covered with a red cloth. A sign informed us that a handbell choir would be playing in about an hour.

"Maybe we can finish up before they start," Dino said hopefully. "Or maybe we won't be able to hear them from the bar."

He wasn't exactly in the Christmas sprit, not unless you thought Ebenezer Scrooge was an appropriate role model.

I said, "The bar?"

"That's where Tack and his wife are meeting us."

"You were pretty sure of me, weren't you?"

"I figured you wouldn't turn down an old friend, even if you hadn't always had a great time doing him favors. And if you didn't want to help, I could always use a free drink. Tack can afford it."

So could Dino, who probably could have bought the hotel if he'd wanted it, though you wouldn't guess it from looking at him. He had on a pair of faded Levi's, and a wrinkled white cotton shirt that he strained at the shoulders because he worked out all the time on exercise equipment he bought after watching infomercials. He was also wearing a pair of scuffed Bass Weejuns that he'd probably bought when he was in college.

I didn't look any better. I was wearing an old sweatshirt with a picture of Bevo, the University of Texas mascot, on the front and a pair of jeans as faded as Dino's. My blue-and-white Etonic running shoes were practically new, though. I thought they gave the outfit a touch of class.

The lobby was full of people who were dressed a lot better than we were. They were considerably older than we were, too, past retirement age, and they were no doubt waiting to go somewhere on one or more of the tour buses. Either that, or listen to the handbell choir.

We made our way through them, hardly attracting a curious glance. Anyone who's been in Galveston more than half an hour knows that the dress code on the Island is pretty lax. Even in a place like the Galvez.

Dino led me past the hotel's restaurant and down a hallway to the bar, which was fronted by huge glass windows that looked out over the seawall and into the Gulf. I could see the Island Retreat, a ramshackle building that extended out over the water on its rickety wooden pier.

I imagined what the building had been like at Christmas forty years ago, when half the high rollers in Texas would have been there to spread a little Christmas cheer and win a little money. Or lose some.

There would have been cars lining the seawall for blocks, big cars like Cadillacs and Buick Roadmasters and Chrysler Imperials. Maybe a Packard or two. There would have been women wrapped in furs, even if the weather had been as warm as it was today. And maybe a national TV star or two.

There was nothing like that now. The street was nearly deserted, and I could see the realtor's sign nailed to the front door of the Island Retreat. The sign was fading now, and I wondered if the building would ever be sold or whether it would just stand there until some wild storm surge dragged it down into the Gulf.

A man stood up at a table near the front of the bar and waved us over. He was big enough to have played football, all right, but he hadn't been in shape for years. He had a belly that jutted out over his belt, and his shirt looked uncomfortably tight. His thick, curly gray hair tumbled over his forehead. His face was puffy, and his voice was a little too loud.

"Hey, Dino," he said. "Come on over."

When we reached the table Dino said, "Tru, this is Tack Kirbo. Tack, Truman Smith."

Kirbo stuck out a hand the size of a Christmas ham, grabbed mine, and tried to crush it.

"Truman Smith," he said. "I guess you don't remember ever seeing me, but I got into a couple of plays against you in a game one day."

I got my hand back before he mangled it. "Dino told me you played with him on the Red Raiders."

Kirbo laughed. "Mostly I just sat on the bench and watched. I wasn't anywhere near the player Dino was. Or you. Hell, you'd have won the Heisman if Dino hadn't torn up your knee for you that day."

"Why don't you introduce your wife?" Dino said.

My knee wasn't his favorite topic of conversation. It was OK for him to mention it to me, but he didn't like anyone else to bring it up. Me neither.

"You must think I have the manners of a hog," Kirbo said, moving aside so that I could see the woman who was sitting in his shadow.

I had a feeling that she sat there a lot. She was much smaller than her husband, and she looked years older. Her face was wrinkled, and her eyes were red, as if she'd been crying recently.

"This is my wife, Janey," Kirbo said. "Janey, this is Dino and

Truman Smith. I've told you about Dino, and in his day Smith was the best damn running back in the Southwest Conference."

There wasn't a Southwest Conference anymore, which was just one more indication of how long ago my day had been. It was something I didn't want to think about much, like my knee.

Janey Kirbo didn't stand up or extend a hand. She didn't even look up at me when she said, "I'm pleased to meet you, Mr. Smith."

Her voice sounded strained, as if it were being squeezed through a very narrow opening.

"Have a seat, have a seat," Kirbo said.

Dino and I pulled out chairs and sat at the table. Almost as soon as we were seated, a young woman with an order pad appeared.

"What'll you have?" Kirbo asked.

I was tempted to ask if Big Red was available, but I knew better, so I just ordered ginger ale. Dino asked for a gin and tonic.

Kirbo said, "Just put it on my tab, honey, and bring me and the little lady two more of the same."

He said it all without any self-consciousness, as if he called all waitresses "honey" and always ordered his wife's drinks without consulting her. I could tell I was going to love working for him.

I looked at Dino, who avoided my eyes. I didn't blame him. It was going to be a long afternoon.

3

DINO AND TACK Kirbo made small talk while we waited for the drinks, something about the Dallas Cowboys' chances of getting to yet another Super Bowl. I didn't pay much attention. I was watching Mrs. Kirbo.

She was looking out the windows, but I didn't think she was seeing anything. Her eyes were as vacant as the Island Retreat.

The drinks came, and I sipped ginger ale while Kirbo told us all how he would have been a better football player if he'd just had the talent to match his desire.

"I tell you," he said, "having to sit on that bench and watch the game was hard on me. I wanted to be in there bangin' heads, but I was always a hair too slow off the ball. I was just as likely to get knocked on my butt as to tackle anybody. One or two plays a game, they'd let me go in, but they just did it to pay me off because I worked so hard in practice. A little reward for bein' a good boy, you could call it. I think if we'd ever had a real solid lead in the fourth quarter, I'd have gotten in for a whole series, maybe two, but in those days we never got that far ahead. The team's a lot better now, though."

I didn't see what any of this had to do with a missing son. I looked at Dino again.

This time he didn't avoid me. He nodded, turned to Kirbo, and said, "Your son got in a little more playing time at Texas Tech than you did, I hear."

It got very quiet at the table for just a second or two. Tack took a deep breath and let it out slowly. Janey Kirbo continued to stare blankly out the windows. She hadn't touched her drink.

Her husband had nearly finished his. He took the last swallow and said, "I guess we might as well get down to it."

"I think that would be a good idea," Dino said.

"But we need more drinks first," Kirbo said, signaling the waitress.

We made more small talk until the drinks arrived and Kirbo dived into his like a man who'd just run a marathon across the Mojave. His wife looked at him, looked at her drink, and looked back out the window.

"All right," Kirbo said to me when he came up for air, half his drink already gone. "How much do you know about the situation?"

I shrugged. "Not much. Your son was here for spring break, he disappeared, he hasn't been found."

"That about says it all," Kirbo told me. "I guess you want more details than that, though."

"You guess right."

"I figured. OK, here's the deal. Randall—that's my boy's name, Randall—he and some friends were down here for spring break, like you said. They went to some parties probably, and I expect they drank some."

He looked at his wife, who gave no sign that she noticed, then back at me.

"There's no harm in drinking," he said, and paused as if he expected someone to contradict him. When no one did, he said, "Not if you do it in moderation."

I wondered whether he was defending his son or himself, but I didn't ask. Since no one seemed inclined to challenge his assumption, he went on.

"Anyway, Randall wasn't much of a drinker. He liked to have fun, but he wasn't ever the kind of a boy to get in trouble. Not in high school, not in college, not ever."

I thought I might as well say something. "But he disappeared."

"Yeah. He disappeared. And nobody knows how or why, least of all your Galveston cops."

I started to tell him they weren't my cops. They didn't belong to anyone, though at one time they had pretty much belonged to Dino's uncles. That was another thing that had changed.

"Tell us about the cops," I said.

"They looked for Randall," Kirbo said. "Or at least that's what they told us. They said they looked hard. But they didn't find him."

"They looked hard," Dino said. I must have seemed surprised at his defense of the police, because he said, "Well, they did. It's not just bad for their reputation when something like that happens. It's bad publicity, and that means it's bad for tourism. See?"

I saw. If word got around that there were mysterious unsolved disappearances here, pretty soon the tourists would find somewhere else to go, and the spring breakers would move on down the coast to Corpus Christi and South Padre, where a lot of them were going already, taking all their nice tourist dollars along with them.

"You mean there was pressure on the police?" I said.

Dino nodded. He didn't say how he knew, but he didn't have to. If he said it, he knew. He might not have had as many ears in high places as his uncles had once had, but he still had plenty.

"And they looked everywhere?"

"Everywhere," Kirbo said. "They said they covered this island with a fine-tooth comb."

"Did your son have any reason to disappear?"

Kirbo looked offended. "What does *that* mean?"

"It means, how were his grades? What was his status with his coaches? Was his girlfriend pregnant?"

Kirbo's face, already a little red, got redder. He gripped the edge of the table with both hands, and for just a fraction of a second I thought he might stand up and slug me. He didn't, though, which may have had something to do with the fact that I was in better shape than he was. Or maybe not.

He said, "You shouldn't talk about a boy like that, not in front of his mother."

As far as I could tell, his mother hadn't even heard me.

"Sorry. It's something that had to be said."

He didn't appear convinced, but I didn't let it worry me. I took a sip of ginger ale and looked at him.

He relaxed his grip on the table and gulped down the rest of his drink. His wife still hadn't touched hers, or said a word.

"I suppose you got a copy of the police report," I said.

"Yes," Mrs. Kirbo said, surprising me. She picked up a canvas bag from the floor and pulled out a thick manila folder. "Here it is."

I took the folder, but I didn't look inside. I laid it on the table and said, "What did the police find out?"

"Not a damn thing," Kirbo said. He tipped his empty glass in the general direction of the report. "What you said a while ago about Randall? How he came down here, disappeared, and hasn't been found? That's what it says."

"If there was pressure on the police to do a good job, they would have done everything possible to find your son," I said. "Even without the pressure, they would have done everything they could. They have the men and the resources to do a lot more than I can. So what makes you think I'm going to find out anything they didn't?"

"Because somebody's lying to them," Kirbo told me.

"Oh," I said, and waited.

Kirbo's theory, expressed with entirely too much hand waving and leaning toward me across the table, was that someone knew something. He wasn't sure who it was, or what they knew, but he was convinced that someone knew what had happened to Randall.

"Maybe his roommate," Kirbo said, leaning back in his chair, much to my relief. "Chad Peavy. He was one of the friends Randall came down here with."

"He's at Texas Tech?" I said.

"No. He flunked out in the spring semester and didn't go back this fall. He's living in Houston with his parents. It's all in that report you've got."

"All right," I said. "Who else?"

"Who else, what?"

"Who else is lying?"

Kirbo looked around the bar for our waitress. I could tell that he wanted another drink. He wanted it a lot. He didn't see the waitress, so he turned back to me.

"Hell, I don't know who's lying. That's why I'm hiring you. To find out."

"You haven't hired me yet," I said.

Mrs. Kirbo looked away from the windows and into my eyes.

"Please," she said. "Help us."

"He will," Dino said, giving me a hard look. "Won't you, Tru?"

I thought about it for a minute, wondering whether Dino had known Mrs. Kirbo when they were college students. And wondering whether I'd have the nerve to ask him.

"I'll try," I said finally. "But I can't make any promises."

Mrs. Kirbo tried to smile and almost made it. "Thank you."

"Don't mention it," I said.

4

DINO DIDN'T HAVE much to say as we drove back to my—OK, his—
house. Dino was in a pretty good mood because we'd managed to get
out of the hotel before the bell choir began playing. He turned on the
radio and punched the button for the Houston oldies station, and we
listened to the usual tunes. My theory is that they have a list with
about a hundred songs on it, and deejays aren't allowed to play anything else. As far as their programmer is concerned, the only song
Roy Orbison ever recorded was "Pretty Woman."

When I was getting out of the car, Dino said, "I hope you can do
something for them, Tru."

I ducked down and stuck my head inside. " 'Them'?"

He squirmed a little on the seat. "Why are you saying it like that?"

"No reason."

"You were always a smart-ass, Tru. Even in high school."

"So you keep reminding me."

"Only because it's true."

My neck was beginning to hurt, so I got back inside the car and
sat down.

"You knew her in college, didn't you?" I said.

He didn't have to ask who I meant. "You guessed, huh?"

"I'm a trained detective, and we trained detectives don't like the
word 'guess.' We prefer 'logical deduction.' "

"Yeah. I'll bet you do."

"So are you going to tell me or not?"

"There's not much to tell. I knew her a lot better than I knew Tack, let's put it that way."

"So I logically deduced."

Dino stared out through the windshield. Where he was parked there wasn't much to see, just the front porch. The house itself was camouflaged by all the bushes that grew so closely around it that it was hard to see it from the road. The Gulf breeze was whipping their branches against the bricks and the windowpanes.

After a while, Dino said, "I went out with her a time or two. But then she started seeing Tack. He was a little bit more of a solid citizen than I was."

"A time or two?"

"Maybe three or four. I wasn't counting."

"Sure."

I didn't say anything for a few seconds. Both of us stared at the porch. Nameless sped across it in hot pursuit of something I couldn't see, maybe one of the geckos that lived in the bushes. Or maybe it was nothing at all. Maybe he was just running for the sheer joy of it, though he was getting a little old for that.

"He's not exactly a solid citizen now," I said. "Tack, that is."

Dino nodded. "He drinks a little. But he's got money that he made the old-fashioned way, in the West Texas oil fields. His daddy was in the business to begin with, but it was Tack that hit it lucky. He was just getting started when that oil shortage came along in the seventies."

"No one mentioned a ransom note," I said.

"There wasn't one. This isn't a kidnapping, Tru. Something funny's going on."

I had a strong sense of déjà vu, and I thought again about the time Dino's daughter had disappeared. I hadn't mentioned it the first time I'd thought of it, and I didn't mention it this time, either.

"Maybe he just didn't want to go home again," I said. "Lots of tension there."

"You noticed."

"Trained detective, remember? We're observant as well as logical."

"Right."

There was something else very familiar about the situation, and it wasn't as touchy as the bit about Dino's daughter, not quite, anyway, so I thought I might as well say something about it.

"You know, getting involved with old girlfriends isn't always a good idea. They might not be the way we remembered them."

"Not everyone's like you, Tru. In the first place, I'm not getting involved with an old girlfriend. And in the second place, she's married. And in the third place, I'm still seeing Evelyn."

"I just wanted to be sure I knew where we stood," I said.

"Well, now you know."

"All right." I got out of the car again. "You want to come in?"

"I think I'll go on home, work out a little. Maybe watch a little TV."

I knew he was eager to get back. He'd been out of the house a lot longer than he liked. I tightened my grip on the copy of the police file as the breeze flapped my sweatshirt and ruffled my hair. I smelled salt and sand and seaweed.

"I'll call you," I said.

"You do that."

I shut the car door, and as I watched the big old Pontiac crunch away down the oyster-shell road, I wondered what I'd gotten myself into this time.

5

I'D BEEN READING from a collection of John O'Hara's Gibbsville stories when Dino had come over to talk to me about the Kirbo disappearance. Not too many people read O'Hara these days, which, for me, was part of his appeal. The other part of his appeal was that he wrote good stories.

I didn't go back to the stories, though, good as they were. I had something else to read. So I put the Kingston Trio's *The Twelfth Month of the Year* on the CD player and sat in the broken-down recliner to look over the police report.

Tack Kirbo had been right. There wasn't much in it. I could tell from reading it that the investigating officer, Bob Lattner, had never developed much interest in finding Randall Kirbo, no matter what Dino had said about the pressure on the police. His interviews with Randall's friends were perfunctory at best, and he had simply accepted everything they'd said with hardly any probing or follow-up. Oh, Lattner had tried to make things look good, all right; he'd checked several times to see if Randall had used his credit card, which he hadn't. Lattner had even gone to Lubbock to do the interviews, but I could tell his heart wasn't in it. His conclusion, based on his "experience and instinct," was that Randall Kirbo had dropped out of sight for reasons of his own and that he hadn't come to any harm.

He might even have been right, but Randall's parents didn't think so, and it was possible that their experience and instincts were just as pertinent as Lattner's.

I closed the file and looked at the photo of Randall that his mother had given me before I left the Galvez. It had been taken for his high school yearbook when he was a senior, and he looked uncomfortable in his jacket and tie, as if the collar of his white dress shirt were a little too tight. It probably was. He was the kind who'd find it difficult to get a collar big enough to fit. He had wide eyes and his father's curly hair, but his face wasn't puffy like Tack's. It was lean and angular but softened by a crooked grin that revealed a chipped front tooth. The All-American Boy.

I wondered where he was now, but I wasn't sure I wanted to be the one to find out. I'd told Mrs. Kirbo I'd try to help, however, so I would.

As it happened, there was a place I could start. I had run into Bob Lattner a couple of times during my short stint at working in the bondsman's office. Lattner probably wouldn't tell me anything, but I thought I might be able to convince him to meet me and talk things over.

Tack Kirbo had also provided me with Chad Peavy's Houston address, and it wouldn't be too much trouble to drive up and have a talk with him. After talking to both him and Lattner, I could most likely use my experience and instinct to come to the same conclusion Lattner had reached. Then I could call the whole thing off.

Except that I wouldn't do that, of course. It wasn't that I felt that I owed anyone anything, it's just that for some reason I can't bring myself to do a job halfway, as Lattner had done. Sometimes I think I'd be better off if I could.

Nameless scratched on the screen door, and I went to let him in. It was dark outside, and I looked at my black plastic digital watch: 6:32. I'd been reading for longer than I'd thought. The Kingston Trio had been silent for a long time now.

I opened the door, and Nameless ran directly to his food dish. I'm pretty sure that the only reason he tolerates my company is that I'm a reliable source of Tender Vittles, which is fine with me. I don't mind buying friendship when it's cheap. I opened a packet of seafood supper and dumped it in the bowl. Nameless began to eat, purring at the same time. I don't know how he did it, but I thought it was a neat trick.

I found a can of Hormel vegetarian chili to fix for myself. It was my kind of food—from the can to the microwave to the table in about five minutes. It tasted OK, too, but I didn't purr while I ate it.

By the time I'd finished and washed my bowl, it was too late to talk to Bob Lattner, so I took the Kingston Trio off the CD player and put on Elvis's *If Every Day Were Like Christmas*, which is the only other holiday album I own. Then I flopped down in the recliner and spent the rest of the evening reading more O'Hara.

After a while Nameless came in and went to sleep on the throw rug under the coffee table. The charms of Elvis singing about a blue Christmas were lost on him. Around eleven o'clock I decided that Nameless had the right idea, so I went to bed.

I don't know whether Nameless dreamed or not, sleeping there on the rug, but I dreamed of running all night long, although I'm pretty sure I never got anywhere. When I woke up the next morning, I was already tired, and the day hadn't even started yet.

Tired or not, I went out for an early morning jog. The sky was covered with low clouds, and the fields that I ran past were thick with fog. The sun would burn it off soon enough, but just then it was almost as if I were running through a fine, gray mist. Droplets clung to my sweatshirt and stuck in my hair. I had to wipe water off my face.

I live on the west end of the Island, between the end of the seawall and the upscale developments, and I went a mile or so without seeing another soul before my knee began to hurt. When I turned to go back home, a big heron lifted off a pool of water about twenty yards away and soared off into the fog without a sound, like a pterodactyl's ghost.

Nameless was watching for me at the door when I got back. He'd spent the night under the coffee table, and now he was ready for breakfast. Seafood supper didn't seem appropriate, but it was all I had. He didn't seem to mind.

I had shredded wheat with skim milk. I was trying to avoid covering my belt buckle the way Tack Kirbo did. While I ate, I listened to the news station on AM radio. Traffic was backed up from Houston almost to Stafford by an accident on the Southwest Freeway, which was really Highway 59, though for some reason I never understood, no one who lives in Houston ever calls it that. I was glad I didn't have to drive to work in Houston every day. For that matter, I was glad I didn't have to drive to work anywhere.

After I finished the shredded wheat, I washed out the bowl and left it in the sink. Nameless jumped up on the counter and leaned over to see if I'd left any water in the bowl. I hadn't, but he licked the bowl anyway.

"Now cut that out," I told him. "It's not sanitary. You might catch some disease."

He ignored me, as usual, but when I started toward him, he jumped down and ran to the door. I let him out so he could terrorize the geckos, which reminded me that it might be a good idea to check my cereal bowl for lizard parts that might have dribbled out of his mouth. There didn't appear to be any, so I figured I was safe from contagion.

I took a shower and pulled on a clean short-sleeved sweatshirt and a pair of faded jeans that I'd worn only once or twice since their last washing. Then I gave Bob Lattner a call.

6

LATTNER DIDN'T WANT to see me, not then, not later that morning, and, I got the distinct impression, not ever. I finally persuaded him to talk to me by offering to buy him lunch. I suggested the Chinese restaurant across from the police station, but he said that he preferred the drugstore, which was fine with me. I knew which drugstore he meant.

"Twelve o'clock?" I asked.

"Make it eleven-thirty," he said.

He had a hard voice that sounded as if he'd practiced it on felons for years. It probably didn't have any more effect on them than it had on me, however; most of them were used to harder voices than his. So was I.

"And good luck finding a parking spot," he added before hanging up.

I wondered what he meant by that, and then it dawned on me: Dickens on the Strand. The east end of the Island would be a foot lower in the water, thanks to the weight of all the extra tourists.

I killed the hours until eleven-thirty by doing a few background checks and by searching some of the electronic databases I had access to for any information on Randall Kirbo. I didn't find a thing, but I wasn't disappointed; I hadn't really expected to.

At a little after eleven I got in my blue-and-white Chevy S-10 truck and drove to town. I wasn't worried about parking. I was pretty sure I knew where there would be a few vacant spots, and I was right.

I parked in the police station lot. There were cars lining the streets and parked everywhere there was anything resembling a spot for them, but no one was willing to take a chance on parking in a cop's place. All the places in the lot were reserved for employees, and I wouldn't have parked there myself under ordinary circumstances. But today I was willing to take a chance.

I got out of the Chevy and walked to the drugstore. It was only a couple of blocks, but the sidewalks were jammed. I must have passed a thousand people on their way to the Strand. Only a few of them were dressed in costumes. I spotted a chimney sweep, a Tiny Tim wearing headphones and carrying a disc player, and a couple of guys who might have been trying to pass as David Copperfield. I suspected that they were awfully warm in their Victorian attire. The fog was long gone, and the sun was bearing down. It must have been nearly eighty degrees, and the humidity was so high that I could feel moisture accumulating under my sweatshirt. It was more like spring than the middle of the winter, but I wasn't complaining.

I walked past a used-book store where two men sat over a chessboard. A very large black dog was asleep in the window. The drugstore was next door, and I went inside. It was a relief to get away from the crowd. Lattner was already there, sitting on a red vinyl-topped stool at the counter that formed a square in the middle of the floor.

The drugstore consisted of one large, high-ceilinged room. The counter took up most of it, but there were display cases that held souvenirs and collectibles like old magazines and movie star photos. The walls were covered with advertising signs, most of them as old as the magazines. A woman with brown hair and wise eyes was behind the counter, and a man with eyes just a little less wise was sweeping the floor with a push broom.

"Crowded out there?" the woman asked me.

"Just a little," I said.

"I wouldn't go out there for a hundred bucks. I just stay in here till it's time to go home, and then I leave. I don't want anything to do with a crowd like that."

I knew what she meant. The crowd would be so thick on the Strand that you couldn't walk where you wanted to. You'd just have to go wherever the ebb and flow of the herd took you.

"I don't blame you," I said. "How's the barbecue plate today?"

"It's good," she said. "But then, it's good every day."

I sat down by Lattner. He was snake-skinny; his belt size must have been about twenty-eight. He had a hatchet face, black hair that he combed straight back, and black eyes that looked right at you. His sports coat must have been ten years old, and it was about one size too big for him. Maybe he'd lost weight some time during the last decade.

"Barbecue all right with you?" I asked him.

"That's what I came for," he said in that hard voice of his. "That and the potato salad."

"Make it two," I said, and the woman turned away to fix the plates. The sweeper disappeared somewhere into the back. Maybe there was another room after all.

Lattner didn't seem inclined to talk, but I figured that since I was buying lunch he might as well earn it.

"About the Kirbo case," I said.

"Nothing to it," Lattner said. "The kid came down here, and he never went home. No evidence of foul play. He was probably tired of college and didn't want to face the folks at home. Case closed."

The woman set two glasses of water in front of us. "Get you anything else to drink?"

"Water's just fine with me," I said, but Lattner wanted iced tea. Probably because I was paying.

"The case isn't really closed," I said. "Kirbo's still missing."

Lattner tilted back his head and took a drink of water. His Adam's apple was the size of a golf ball.

"Just a manner of speaking," he said, setting his glass on the counter. "It's an open case, sure, technically open. But it might as well be closed. No one's going to find that kid. I've talked to his friends; they don't know where he went or what happened to him. I've talked to his parents; they don't know, either. He hasn't used his credit cards, he hasn't phoned home, and he hasn't turned up on *America's Most Wanted*. He doesn't want to be found, and no one's going to find him."

"I am," I said, and immediately regretted giving Lattner an opening.

He didn't hesitate to take it. "Bullshit. You couldn't find your fanny with a flashlight. I've heard about you, Smith."

I didn't ask what he'd heard or where he'd heard it. Galveston is a small town. Word gets around. What interested me was why he wanted to make me angry.

"That's pretty funny, that flashlight bit," I said. "I remember laughing a lot when I heard it the first time. About thirty years ago."

"I know you're a smart-ass, too, so you don't have to waste your time proving it. And I know one other thing. I know you have a habit of messing around in things that aren't any of your business. I don't really care about that, not unless you start messing around in something I'm involved with, like the Kirbo case. If you do that, you're really going to piss me off."

Our barbecue arrived about that time, and Lattner had worked himself up to such a state of self-righteous dudgeon that I figured he'd just get off the stool and leave. I was wrong, though. He turned his attention to the food and started to eat with a dedication to the job that even Nameless would have admired.

I didn't watch him for long. I ate my own barbecue. The sauce was just tangy enough, and the potato salad wasn't too sweet. I took my time. Lattner was finished long before I was, but for some reason he didn't leave. He got up and walked around the drugstore, looking in all the display cases as if he might actually be interested in buying a black-and-white glossy of James Dean.

When I'd finished sopping up the last of the barbecue sauce with a piece of bread, Lattner came back over to the counter and sat beside me again.

"If that kid could have been found, I'd have found him," he said. "And I'm twice the investigator you are. So why don't you just go back and sit in your little house and listen to your records and keep your nose where it belongs?"

"Compact discs," I said.

That bothered him. "Huh?"

"Compact discs, not records. I don't play records; I play compact discs."

"I don't care if you play goddamn tiddledywinks. I don't want you messing in my cases."

"You don't like me much, do you, Lattner?"

"I don't like you at all." He slid off the stool and started for the door. Just before he got there, he turned back and said, "Thanks for lunch."

I had to laugh at that. The counter woman was picking up our plates, and she said, "Swell guy. He a good friend of yours?"

"Not yet," I said. "But he will be. I have a way of winning people over."

She stacked my plate on top of Lattner's. "I'll just bet you do," she said.

7

I WAS PRETTY sure who Lattner had been talking to about me, a cop named Gerald Barnes. He'd probably checked with Barnes after I'd called, knowing that I'd had dealings with Barnes on a couple of other cases, something that wasn't any big secret around the cop shop. I'd thought Barnes had begun to develop a sort of grudging respect for me because of some of the work I'd done. Obviously I'd been wrong, however, and I didn't think it would do me any good to try to get anything more out of Lattner. He appeared to be the kind of cop who had no regard for people he considered amateurs, meaning anyone who didn't carry a badge. I wasn't going to be able to impress him with a list of my successes. All he was interested in was my failures, and there were more than enough of those.

I stood outside the drugstore and thought for about a tenth of a second about walking down to the Strand and looking things over. I could hear a band, and I knew that there was a parade every day about this time. With an elephant or two, even. Then I thought again about the crowds and started toward my car.

I passed a boy about ten gnawing on a giant turkey leg. His father and mother walked along beside him, and their turkey legs were even bigger than his. I wasn't quite sure exactly what the connection between Dickens and turkey legs was supposed to be, but they seemed to be enjoying them. I've never been tempted to try one.

When I got to my truck, I saw that I was in luck. No vindictive city employee had ticketed me. I decided that since I was in the neighborhood, more or less, I'd drive by Sally Western's house and pay her a visit. Sally had been around for a long time, and she knew as much as anyone in Galveston about what happened on the Island. Also, she enjoyed talking. Maybe she'd heard something about Randall Kirbo. There weren't many people who paid Sally a visit these days, and she was usually glad to see me, even if the only times I dropped by were when I needed information from her.

I stopped off at a liquor store and picked up a bottle of Sally's favorite wine—Mogen David. Sally's family was among the Island's elite, and her personal fortune was somewhere in the neighborhood of thirty million dollars, but she had simple tastes, which was just as well for me. I couldn't afford the kind of wine that most multimillionaires no doubt preferred, and I wasn't even sure that the stores I went to would have it in stock.

When I got to Sally's house, I parked in the street and climbed the steps to her front door. Almost as soon as I knocked the door was opened by John, the old black man who'd been working for Sally for as long as I could remember. He wasn't as old as she was, however. Hardly anyone was as old as Sally, who must have been getting close to a hundred.

"Hello, Mr. Truman," John said.

"Hello, John." I handed him the wine. "Is Miss Sally in today?"

"Yes, sir, she is. She's in the parlor, and I know she'd be glad to see you."

He moved back to let me in, and I followed him to the parlor. He always announced visitors, no matter how well Sally knew them.

"Come in, Truman," she said in a voice that belied her fragile appearance.

I stepped inside and looked around. The parlor hadn't changed at all since my last visit, but then, I suspected that it hadn't changed in the last fifty years, or even longer. There were two cane-bottomed rocking chairs, one for Sally and one for visitors. There was a small wooden table beside Sally's chair. An old piano stood against one wall, and on the wall I could see the dim mark that showed how high the waters of the flood of 1900 had risen in the room.

Sally's appearance hadn't changed, either. She was dressed all in black, just as she'd been the last time I'd seen her. Her hair was just as white, and her eyes were just as sharp and alert.

"I don't suppose you came by just to see how an old woman is doing, did you?" she asked.

"No," I said, feeling a little guilty. "I don't suppose you could say that."

"That's good, then. It means that you have some gossip for me."

I needn't have felt guilty. Sally loved gossip, as she called it, and she loved talking about my cases. Whenever I got one that required her help, I made another trip to her house after it was over to let her know how things had turned out, a courtesy she always appreciated.

"I don't really have any gossip," I said just as John came into the room.

As usual he had the Mogen David on a silver tray with two crystal glasses. Neither Sally nor I spoke as he poured the wine. I thanked him when he handed me my glass, though I took it only out of politeness. I can drink Big Red, but Mogen David is different.

Sally, on the other hand, didn't hesitate. She took a large swallow and smiled with satisfaction.

"It's very nice of you to bring this, Truman," she said. "It does an old woman good to have a touch of wine for her stomach's sake."

"I think that's what St. Paul said."

"You are correct. And how right he was." She took another swallow. "Now tell me what you came here for. Have you been to Dickens on the Strand?"

"Not exactly," I said. "I was close, though."

"Closer than I would like to be, I'm sure. I'm afraid the crowds would simply run over and trample me."

I told her that I didn't really think that was true. Sally might have been small, but she wasn't the type to let anyone run over her.

"You're flattering me, but don't worry. I can accept flattery gracefully. But we've gotten away from your reason for coming by. Please tell me now."

I told her what little I knew about Randall Kirbo and what seemed to me to be his mysterious disappearance. It didn't take very long.

"I was hoping that you might have heard something about it," I said. "Nearly anything would help."

She had already finished her wine, so I walked over to her chair and poured her a second glass.

"You've hardly touched your own," she said.

"I'll get to it. Right now, I'm more interested in anything you might have heard about Randall Kirbo."

"I'm sorry to say that I haven't heard a thing," she said, sipping more delicately at the wine than she had earlier. "I don't seem to be hearing as much as I used to. Or maybe I'm simply forgetting it."

I said that I doubted that very seriously. "You've never forgotten a single thing. I'd be willing to bet that you've got the entire history of the Island in that head of yours."

She smiled. "I don't have quite as much faith in my memory as you do, but you might not be far wrong."

"Nothing in there about a young man disappearing during last year's spring break, though."

"Nothing at all, I'm afraid."

"Well, that's all right. I'm glad I got to come by and see you, anyway."

"So am I. It's always nice to talk to you. Would you be interested in anything else that happened at spring break?"

If she wanted to talk for a bit longer, that was all right with me. Her stories were always interesting, whether they had anything to do with the job I was doing or not.

"Like what?" I asked.

She looked into her half-full glass. "It has nothing to do with a disappearance, I'm afraid."

"That's all right," I said. "I like gossip almost as much as you do."

That wasn't quite true, but sometimes a little white lie doesn't hurt anything. I thought this was probably one of those times.

"What does it have to do with?" I asked.

"It has to do with something being found, which I suppose is the opposite of what you're asking about."

"Don't tell me that someone found Lafitte's treasure," I said, "and that no one told me about it. I'd really hate that. I've been looking for that treasure since I was six."

Sally laughed. It was a short, dry sound, more like a couple of wheezes, but it was a laugh.

"Half the people born on the Island have been looking for that treasure since they were six," she said. "Not to mention the people who come here from other places to look. I only wish it were something like that. I'd love to be alive when that treasure is found. If it ever is."

I didn't think it ever would be. Lafitte's treasure was one of the Island's legends that everyone wanted to believe but no one really did. At least not for very long after about the age of six.

"If they didn't find treasure," I said, "what did they find?"

"Something much less pleasant than treasure," Sally said. "But possibly more interesting in its own way. And something that a person like you should have heard about."

"A person like me?"

"Someone who has an interest in the unusual and the bizarre."

"I'm not sure I'm following you. What exactly was it that they found?"

Sally decided that she had teased me long enough. She put her crystal glass on the wooden table and said, "What they found was a body."

MY FIRST REACTION was that maybe I should spend more time reading the Galveston *Daily News*, which billed itself as "Texas's Oldest Newspaper," a title that occasionally inspired some of the locals to suggest that it be shortened to "Texas's Oldest News."

"I didn't hear about any body being found," I said.

Sally wasn't surprised. "It's no wonder. You hardly ever leave that house of yours unless you're working on something for Dino. I worry about you. Dino, too."

It wasn't the first time she'd mentioned that. She thought that both of us should get out more because we were just as reclusive as she was, without having age as an excuse.

"Whatever happened to that woman you were seeing?" she asked. "Cathy Macklin?"

I looked at the floor. It was a nice floor, polished hardwood, but there was nothing there that would answer her question.

"I'm not sure," I said. "It just ended, I guess."

"Hah. Things don't 'just end.' They end for a reason."

"You're right," I admitted. "But I'm not sure I know what the reason was."

That was another one of those little white lies. I thought I knew the reason, all right, but if I tried to explain it to Sally, she'd just think that it confirmed her suspicions about me. And it probably did.

Cathy and I liked each other. We enjoyed being together. We

even had some of the same interests. But that was as far as it went, mainly because I wasn't willing to make the effort to take it any farther. I was filled with a powerful sense of inertia, and it took something special to get me moving. Usually that something was Dino. If it hadn't been for him, I would most likely have spent all my days listening to CDs, working at the computer, and reading out-of-print books.

Oddly enough, I worried much more about Dino than about myself, and I tried to get him out of his house more often. It was easy enough for me to see what he needed to do. It was a little harder for me to see that I had some of the same problems that he did, or maybe I thought that I had better reasons. Dino had the legend of his uncles, which he'd chosen not to live up to. I had my failure to find my sister when she really needed me. Neither of us liked to face those things.

I realized that neither Sally nor I had said anything for a while, and I looked up at her. She was watching me calmly, rocking her chair quietly back and forth.

"I didn't really come here to talk about me," I said.

Sally nodded. "I know that. It was just something I thought I'd mention. I hope you didn't mind."

"It's OK. Now tell me about that body."

She really didn't know much more about it than I knew about Randall Kirbo. The essential facts were that the body of a young woman, Kelly Davis, had been found by a couple of surfers who'd gone out to catch some waves early one morning on the last Friday of spring break. That would have made it March 20 by my reckoning.

The woman had been floating in the Gulf, only about fifteen yards from shore. The surfers, Jack Munson and Todd Allen, had been paddling on top of the green water near one of the granite jetties when they passed the body. They pulled it to the beach, realized that CPR wasn't going to do a bit of good, and called the police.

"How did she die?" I asked. "Drowning?"

Sally said, "There wouldn't really be much interest in that, now would there?"

I didn't suppose there would be. Drownings weren't exactly everyday occurrences in the Gulf, but they weren't uncommon, either.

"There was no water in her lungs," Sally said. "The police believe that she was put into the Gulf after she died."

"Murder?"

"There were no signs that she had been in a struggle. There were no marks on the body, except for a few scrapes that most likely came from the jetty. She wasn't shot or stabbed or choked or beaten."

"Was a cause of death ever determined?"

Sally shook her head. "I don't believe so. If it was, there hasn't been a mention of it in the paper, and no one has told me about it."

The lack of a mention in the paper didn't prove much, but the fact that no one had told Sally made it pretty certain that no determination had been made. Sally might not get many visitors, but she had a telephone.

"Who was Kelly Davis?" I asked.

"She wasn't from the Island," Sally said. "That's why I mentioned her in the first place. She was here for spring break. She was a student at Southwest Texas State."

But not at Texas Tech, I thought. Still, it was an interesting co-incidence—a young man disappears, a young woman dies. If the two cases were related, or even if the cops only suspected that they were, Lattner's hostility was a little easier to understand.

"The police investigated, of course," I said.

"Of course. A friend of yours was in charge."

"A friend?"

"Gerald Barnes. You've crossed paths with him before, haven't you?"

She knew very well that I had. I'd told her all about the disappearances of Dino's daughter and Outside Harry. In both instances I'd been involved with Barnes.

"I know Barnes," I said. "I might even have to get to know him a little better."

Sally didn't actually rub her hands together, but she gave the impression of doing so.

"I'm sure he'll enjoy that," she said.

"Has anyone told you lately that you're an evil old woman?"

Sally laughed her dry laugh again. "How I wish that were true. I haven't had the opportunity to be evil in decades."

"Sure you haven't. Now what else do you know that you haven't told me?"

Sally thought for a second. "Well, you haven't asked me what she was wearing."

"Right. So tell me, what was she wearing?"

"Nothing unusual. Just shorts and some kind of T-shirt with an advertisement on it."

"What kind of advertisement?"

"I don't know. Could that mean anything?"

Probably not, I thought. Everyone these days seemed perfectly willing to pay twelve bucks for a T-shirt that advertised some product or clothing line. Not only were the products and clothing lines making money, they were getting all kinds of free advertising. It seemed like a good racket to me.

"I don't know about the advertisement," I said. "But she wasn't wearing a bathing suit. That might mean something."

Sally agreed. "That's another reason the police believe the girl was put in the water after her death. She obviously wasn't out for a swim."

"How long had she been in the water?"

Sally hardly ever drank more than two glasses of wine during one of my visits, though I was certain that she had more after I left. Now she looked at the wine bottle and then back at me. I can take a hint, so I got up and filled her glass. My own glass, still half full, sat on the floor by my chair.

"You've still hardly touched your wine," Sally said as I poured.

"I'm not very thirsty," I said. I went back to my chair. "Did the cops have any idea how long the body had been in the water? Any estimate of the time of death?"

"I've never been sure just how such things are determined." She took a dainty sip of Mogen David. "At any rate, they believe that she'd been in the water only a few hours. Most likely she was put in only a short time before she was found, probably not long before dawn. She must have died a few hours earlier."

"What about her family and friends? Did anyone find out where she'd been, what she'd been doing, and who she'd been doing it with?"

"You really must think I know a lot more than I do, Truman, if you think I know all of that. Even my sources aren't *that* good. In fact, I don't know any of it. I suppose that you'll have to talk to your police friend, Mr. Barnes, about it."

I could think of several other things I'd rather do. Some of them weren't even especially pleasant things. But they were better than going to see Barnes.

"Why should I talk to him?" I asked. "I'm not working on that case. I'm looking for a kid named Randall Kirbo."

"You don't find it intriguing that he disappeared at about the same time a young woman's body was found?"

"We don't know exactly when he disappeared. And we certainly don't know that he had any connection with Kelly Davis."

She looked disappointed in me. "And we don't know that no one has talked to the police about her death, do we? But it seems very likely that no one has. Two strange events during the same week, and no one will talk about either one of them. I find that peculiar."

So did I, but I was still hoping there was no connection.

"Don't you?" Sally asked.

I knew very well what she meant, but I said, "Don't I what?"

"Don't you find it peculiar?"

"Yes," I said. I sighed. "Yes, I guess I do."

Somewhere inside my head I heard Dino's voice: "It'll be different this time."

Sure it would. I'd hardly gotten started, and already it seemed pretty likely that there was a dead body involved.

Goddamn that Dino, anyway.

9

"THERE'S ABSOLUTELY NO connection between the disappearance of Randall Kirbo and the death of Kelly Davis," Gerald Barnes told me, so unconvincingly that I was immediately certain he thought there was.

We were sitting at his desk in the police station. I'd taken the same parking spot I'd used earlier, knowing that I was pressing my luck but hoping that everyone was too busy watching the money changing hands at the turkey-leg booths down on the Strand to give me a ticket. I was at least lucky enough to have caught Barnes in the building. He had too much seniority to pull guard duty.

"How do you know there's no connection?" I asked.

Barnes had thinning brown hair and wore glasses with heavy plastic frames, the kind you don't see very often these days. Buddy Holly would have been proud. He pushed his glasses up on his nose and looked at me. He didn't answer my question.

"Bob Lattner asked me about you earlier," he said. "You know what I told him?"

"That I was an expert detective who'd solved a couple of really tough cases for you?"

"That's part of your trouble, Smith. You think too much of yourself. You didn't solve those cases. I solved them. You just hung around and got in the way."

If that was the way he wanted to look at it, I wasn't going to argue with him. It wouldn't do any good, and I think we both knew better, anyway. Even if he didn't, I certainly did.

"What's the other part of my trouble?" I asked.

"You're a smart-ass."

I was beginning to think that was a unanimous opinion among all my acquaintances. That didn't mean they were right, of course.

"Thanks for sharing that with me," I said. "Now, let's get back to what we were talking about, the nonexistent connection between the disappearance of Randall Kirbo and the death of Kelly Davis."

"Someone might have hired you to look into the disappearance, Smith," Barnes told me, "but that doesn't give you the right to poke around in any other ongoing investigations."

His glasses had slipped again. I started to suggest that he go in and have them adjusted, but I decided he wouldn't appreciate the advice. So I kept it to myself.

Instead, I said, "Let's just pretend for a second that while I'm trying to find out what happened to Kirbo, I happen to discover that he knew Kelly Davis. What then?"

"Then you inform me. I'll take it from there."

"You haven't taken it any great distance so far."

Barnes took off his glasses and set them on the desk. His eyes suddenly looked smaller. He pinched the bridge of his nose and leaned back in his chair.

"You're right about that," he said.

I knew then that he was weakening. Or maybe he'd just been setting me up. Maybe he'd been planning to tell me all along.

"Just tell me what you do know," I said. "We can help each other on this. We've done it before."

He picked up the glasses and slid them back on. He looked around to see if anyone was listening to us, but no one was. There was hardly anyone else there.

"What I'm about to tell you?" he said.

"What about it?"

"I didn't say it."

"Of course you didn't."

"All right. We think there's a connection between Kirbo and Davis, all right. Hell, we *know* there is. We just can't get anywhere with it. We're getting stonewalled all around."

"But you're going to tell me what the connection is."

"Yes. Not that I think it'll do you any good."

"You never can tell," I said.

"That's right. You might accidentally stumble onto something. Otherwise I'd be keeping my mouth shut."

"You're not, though. So what's the connection?"

"We think that Randall Kirbo did know Kelly Davis, but we can't prove it. We think they met at a party at a beach house, but we're not sure who else was there. We've put a little pressure on a few of the ones we think might know something, but we can't get a thing out of them."

"Why not?"

"The beach house is owned by Big Al Pugh," he said as if that explained it all.

Maybe it did. Big Al was into a little of everything—restaurants, beach property, illegal gambling, prostitution, and drugs—or so it was said. No one had ever proved anything about the illegal stuff, mainly because people who seemed likely to reveal any of Big Al's secrets had a way of turning up missing. No one wanted to mess with Big Al. Not even the police. Certainly not me.

Goddamn that Dino.

"I'm surprised you found anyone who *might* even know something," I said.

"So am I," Barnes admitted. "But we don't have much. We found a couple of kids who didn't know any better, and they said they thought that maybe they'd seen Kirbo and Davis at the party, but they couldn't say whether they were together or not. And the next time we talked to them, they didn't even remember that much."

"Big Al had a little talk with them," I suggested.

"I doubt it. Big Al doesn't talk to anybody, not that way, not these days. I figure it was Henry J."

I wasn't sure what the exact relationship between Henry J. and Big Al was. They might have been partners, or Henry J. might have been just an employee. If anything, Henry J. was bigger and meaner than Al. If that was possible.

"None of that was in the police report Randall Kirbo's father had."

Barnes didn't say anything. He tilted his head back and looked at the ceiling. Well, the report had been only a copy, not anything official.

"What can you give me?" I asked.

He thought about that for a while, then opened a desk drawer and pulled out a folder a lot like the one Tack Kirbo had given me.

"I'm going to take a walk outside," he said. "Get a little fresh air. If you copy anything out of that report, I won't know about it."

That was fine with me. He had a pencil and paper lying on his otherwise clean desk, and I started writing almost before he had taken ten steps. I got the names of the two people who'd said they might have seen Kirbo and Davis at the party and the phone number and address of Davis's parents, who lived in San Antonio.

It wasn't much, and Barnes was back as soon as I'd finished. He took the folder and slid it back into the desk drawer.

"You knew I was coming," I said, folding the paper I'd written on and slipping it in the back pocket of my jeans. "You had the folder ready."

"I thought you might drop by."

"I wasn't invited."

"I told Lattner not to give anything away. I wanted to see if you'd put it together. You did it a lot faster than I thought you would. I wasn't expecting you for a couple of days."

"People like you and Lattner always tend to underrate us expert detectives."

"Maybe. I don't think so."

"I have one other question. Why was Lattner so hostile to me? If you told him you were going to cooperate with me eventually, he didn't have to act like a jerk. Was that part of the test?"

Barnes shook his head. "No. There's something else, something that's not in the report."

I had a feeling I wasn't going to like what he told me, but I asked anyway.

"What?"

"Lattner's related to Kelly Davis. She was his niece."

I thought about that for a while. Then I thought about what might happen if I killed Dino. I figured that no jury in the world would convict me.

10

BY THE TIME I got to Dino's house, I'd decided not to kill him.

I had something worse in mind.

He lived out of sight of the water in a subdivision that might just as well have been in some old neighborhood in Dallas or Ft. Worth. The houses had all been built of light-colored brick fifty or sixty years earlier in a pseudo-English style, and some of them even had ivy growing on the walls. Not Dino's, however. He'd had a little trouble with termites at some time in the past, and the exterminator had advised him to eliminate the ivy, which he'd done immediately.

I had to knock a couple of times before he came to the door.

"Sorry, Tru," he said as I walked past him into the house. "I didn't hear you at first. I was watching this great infomercial with Mark Wilson. Remember him?"

"The magician?"

"That's the guy. He was on TV when we were kids. Now he's selling magic tricks."

"Have you ordered them?"

"Nah. I figure I'm too old to learn something like that. It might be fun, though."

"Not as much fun as what we're about to do right now."

He gave me a puzzled look. "We're going to do something?"

"That's right. We're going fishing. Get your gear together."

"Huh?"

"Your gear. Fishing gear. We're going fishing. Hop to it."

He didn't hop. He just stood there and gawked at me stupidly. I gawked back. I can look just as stupid as the next guy.

He looked away, and his eyes swept over the room, lingering on the oversized TV set where Mark Wilson was showing some balding huckster a dollar bill that folded itself. Wilson didn't look much older than he had thirty years earlier. Maybe he knew more magic than he was selling.

Dino watched the infomercial for a couple of seconds, and then he looked back at me. He said, "I don't like fishing, Tru."

He didn't like getting out of the house, either, and, like a lot of people who're born on the Island, he didn't like being around the water.

"I like fishing," I said.

"Yeah, well, you just go ahead without me. I don't even have a fishing rod."

"I have a spare you can use. Let's go."

He walked over to his couch and sat down. Then he reached out and got his remote control, which looked only a little more complicated than the control panel in a state-of-the-art recording studio, and muted the TV set.

"You're really chapped about something, Tru. You want to talk about it?"

"I guess maybe I do," I said. So I sat down and told him about how I'd spent my day so far.

When I was done, Dino said, "I don't much like dealing with cops."

"I don't much care what you like," I said. "This Kirbo business has turned out to be a lot worse than you made it out to be, and I have to get information where I can. You sure aren't giving it to me."

"You don't think I knew any of that stuff when I asked you to help Tack, do you?"

"I don't know what you knew. All I know is that every single time you ask me to do you a favor, things start getting awfully complicated."

His eyes drifted to the TV set. Mark Wilson was gone, replaced by a couple of men with ties on, sitting at a desk and talking. I had no idea what they might be selling.

"This guy's amazing," Dino said, pointing at the chubbier of the two. "He can read a book in about five seconds and tell you everything that's in it."

"I'm sure that's a useful skill. But you're changing the subject."

"Yeah, I know. That's because you hurt my feelings."

I couldn't believe it. "What the hell are you talking about? I'm the injured party here."

"No, you're not. You don't trust me. That hurts my feelings."

"I trust you, all right. I trust you to get me into more trouble than I can get out of by myself. But this time you're going to help."

"How?"

"By going fishing. Come on."

He punched the remote, and the TV went blank. "OK. If that's the way you want it."

WE DROVE OUT to the house and picked up my fishing tackle, which didn't take long. I don't have a lot of gear, just a couple of old Penn reels, two rods, a bait bucket, and a tackle box full of miscellaneous junk that might come in handy—pliers, weights, leaders, hooks, extra line, a few battered lures.

After I tossed everything in the back of the S-10, we drove to Jody's bait shop on Offatt's Bayou, which is where I usually buy my bait. Jody has squid and mullet and bait shrimp, and he even sells tackle, though not very often judging by the dust on the few lure boxes on his shelves.

"Are we going to fish here?" Dino asked when I parked in front of Jody's shop.

It wouldn't have been a bad idea if fishing had been all I was interested in. The wind wasn't kicking up the water in the bayou much, and several people were fishing nearby and enjoying the mild day.

"No, we're going somewhere else," I said. "We're going to buy some bait here. You can come in with me."

"You don't need me."

"It's part of the deal. You have to come in."

He was a better sport than I might have been under similar circumstances. He got out, I got the bait bucket, and we went inside, where the smell of mullet and shrimp was thick enough to cut with a knife.

"Hello, Jody," I said.

Because I'd once forced Jody to tell me something he didn't want to tell, he didn't trust me anymore than I trusted Dino. But he was still a businessman. He never refused to sell bait to me, though it was obvious he wasn't overwhelmed with joy to see us walk in.

"You know Dino, I think," I said.

"Haven't seen him for years," Jody said. "How you doin', Mr. D.?"

Dino looked around unhappily. "I'm doing all right. How about you, Jody?"

"Just fine." He looked at me. "I think."

"We just came by for some bait," I said. "Dino wants me to take him to Pelican Island. Anything biting over there?"

"Haven't heard. Nice day for it, though. Little windy, but nice and warm."

"Maybe we can catch us a nice flounder or two," I said, setting the bait bucket on the counter. "How about a couple of dozen shrimp?"

Jody caught the shrimp, I paid him, and Dino and I went back to the truck. When he'd slammed the door, Dino said, "Pelican Island?"

"That's right. You heard what Jody said. It's a nice day for it."

"There has to be a better reason than that. I know you're mad at me, but you wouldn't be dragging me to Pelican Island just to punish me, would you?"

"Why not?"

"Because nobody's that big an asshole, not even you."

"I wouldn't be too sure of that," I said.

Dino started to say something, then shut his mouth. Maybe he was revising his opinion of me.

PELICAN ISLAND IS a small island just to the north of Galveston. The Texas legislature, in a fit of unaccustomed generosity, gave it to the city some time around the middle of the nineteenth century, and no one since that time has been quite sure what to do with it. There have been several businesses located there, but none of them has been a raging success. Now it's the home of the maritime branch of Texas A & M University. The campus is the first thing you see after you cross the drawbridge, unless you happen to glance at the ship the school uses for some of its classes.

We weren't on Pelican Island to enroll in school or take an educational trip on an oceangoing vessel, however. We were there to fish at the island's other attraction, Seawolf Park, which is located a couple of miles past the campus. The park is named for a World War II submarine that you can tour there anytime you feel the need to induce a little claustrophobia in yourself.

There's also a destroyer to tour, and out in the channel to the north there's a concrete battleship that was deliberately sunk there. Part of it is clear of the water, and you can get a good look at it if you have a pair of binoculars.

As far as I know, it was the only concrete battleship ever built, and it might have worked out very well if it had ever been used in battle. Unfortunately, we'll never know, since World War II ended the day the battleship was commissioned. It was used for a while as a tanker instead, until it was damaged in a storm, brought to Galveston for repairs, and eventually sunk in the channel when the repairs didn't work out. People have tried for years to figure out constructive ways to use it, from making it into an oyster farm to using it as a resort hotel, but so far nothing has ever been done.

The best fishing is on the side of the island that faces the Strand. I paid the park attendant, parked the truck, and told Dino to get the tackle out of the truck while I looked for a good spot to set up.

Dino didn't move. "I still don't know why the hell you brought me out here. I haven't been on Pelican Island in twenty years, and I don't want to be here now."

"Didn't I tell you? Sally Western says you need to get out of the house more."

"I don't care what Sally Western thinks." He looked around at the park, the people fishing, the ferries plying the water between Galveston and the Bolivar Peninsula, the ships out in the Gulf. "I think I'll just sit here in the truck and wait for you."

"That wouldn't be a very good idea," I said. "I might need your help."

"You won't need my help just to catch a fish."

"Well, maybe not. But I might need your help with someone who's fishing here."

"What are you talking about?"

"You remember where that party was, the one I told you about on the way over, where Randall Kirbo and Kelly Davis were seen?"

"At some beach house."

"Very good. And who owned the beach house?"

"Big Al Pugh," Dino said. And then his eyes widened just a little. "Oh. I get it."

"I thought you might. Now get the tackle while I look around."

"What if you're wrong?"

"Then it wouldn't be the first time, would it?"

"No."

He still didn't want to get out, so I said, "Look at it this way—at least I didn't drag you to the Strand."

He looked across the choppy water of the West Bay to the Island. He couldn't really see the Strand from where we were. There were buildings in the way. But it was easy to imagine the swarms of people there.

"I guess you do like me, after all," Dino said. "Either that, or you really must think you need protection."

"I like you," I said. "I really like you."

"Sally Field. You remember the year she made that speech at the Academy Awards?"

"No," I said. "Now you get the tackle, and I'll go look for Big Al."

11

EVERYONE KNEW THAT Big Al Pugh liked to mingle with the common folk by fishing on Pelican Island, and since today was such a good day for fishing, I was hoping that I'd get lucky. Of course, if Big Al was there, Henry J. would be there, too, which is why I'd brought Dino along. There was no use in my getting beaten to a pulp by myself.

The concrete walk that had been built along the side of the island facing the West Bay was crowded with fisherpersons of all shapes and sizes. As I looked around for Big Al, a kid of about twelve was nearly jerked off the walk and his rod bent double. His father grabbed him by the belt as the kid started cranking on his reel. It took them a few minutes, but the two of them finally got a hubcap-sized flounder close enough to shore for everyone to see it. The father got a dip net and leaned down toward the water to scoop up their catch.

I didn't hang around to see if he landed the fish. By that time I'd spotted Big Al sitting in a sagging aluminum lawn chair about thirty yards farther along the walk. There was no sign of Henry J., however, which I thought was unusual but encouraging. I went back to the truck to get Dino.

He was standing there with the rods and the tackle box in one hand and the bait bucket in the other, looking as if he wished he were back at home with his big-screen TV and his complicated remote control.

"Well?" he said.

"We're in luck."

"You mean Big Al's not here?"

"No, I mean Big Al *is* here. Not only that, but the fish are biting."

For some reason, neither bit of news seemed at all exciting to Dino. He just looked even more depressed, if that was possible.

"What's the matter?" I asked. "Don't you like fish?"

"I like fish just fine if they're in the water. But I don't like catching them, I don't like cleaning them, and I don't like cooking them. If I want to eat fish, I'll go to a restaurant."

I thought about asking him when he'd last been to a restaurant, but there was no use in that. He'd been whenever I'd last forced him out of the house to go to one with me.

"Maybe we won't catch anything," I said.

He looked hopeful. "Maybe. What about Henry J.?"

"I didn't see him."

"That doesn't mean he's not here."

"I know it. Come on. We can't stand around like this all day."

I led the way, and Dino followed. I didn't have to look back to know that he wasn't happy about it. Not only were we out of his house, we were right on the water. In a few seconds, we were going to be within about a foot of it. I don't think Dino had been this close to Galveston Bay in years. A lot of years. No wonder he was uncomfortable.

And, of course, the meeting with Big Al wasn't going to be as much fun as a lot of other things we could have been doing.

Having elective hernia surgery, for instance.

There was a strong breeze, and the water had slopped up on the concrete, making it slick. I had on my running shoes, so I didn't think I was in much danger of slipping. Dino was also wearing running shoes, though I don't think he ever went running. Free weights, an ab machine, and a treadmill were more his style.

Although the walk was crowded, there was plenty of space around Big Al. People were showing their respect, or it might have been fear.

I wasn't afraid, or if I was, I wasn't going to show it. I walked to within a couple of yards of the sagging chair and said, "This looks like a good spot, Dino."

Big Al, who had been staring out at the water, turned to look at me.

"Well, well. Truman Smith. And Dino. I'd heard you were into
fishing lately, Tru, but I didn't know Dino cared for water sports."

It was easy to see where Big Al got her nickname. She was nothing
if not big. And impressive. I don't know whether she'd ever entered
competitive body-building contests, but she certainly could have.
The muscles of her arms and legs looked as if they were composed
of bricks with the edges rounded off, and she looked strong enough
to bend a crowbar the way I might bend a paper clip.

She was wearing a pair of cutoffs and a tight white T-shirt with a
picture of a black automatic pistol held in a two-handed grip. Under
the pistol was written I DON'T DIAL 9-1-1. To tell the truth, I didn't
think she'd need the pistol. Bare hands would be enough of a defense
for her.

She was wearing a white visor that allowed a view of her unnatu-
rally kinky hair, cut short and close to her head in tight, graying curls.
She had a weathered face with watery gray eyes, and a nose that had
been broken at least once. She'd probably run into a door.

Her full first name was Alice, but probably no one had called her
that in thirty years. Well, no one but Henry J. I wondered where he
was. I had been sure from the first that Big Al hadn't come alone, and
the empty chair beside her proved that I was right.

Dino said, "Where's Henry J.?"

"What?" Big Al said. "No 'Hi, Big Al,' no greeting for an old
friend?"

Dino put the tackle and bait bucket down. "Hi, Big Al."

"Hi, yourself. You boys think you're going to catch some fish
today?"

"We might," I said. "Let's bait up, Dino."

I could tell by the look on his face that Dino found the idea of
putting live shrimp on a hook about as appealing as cleaning out a
cat's litter box with his bare hands, so I knelt down by the bait bucket
and got busy.

"Dino's too delicate for that kind of work," Big Al said. She patted
the arm of the empty chair. "Here you go, Dino, have a seat by me
and tell me what's been happening in your life. How long's it been
since we talked, anyway? Five years? Ten?"

Dino looked at the empty chair, but he didn't make a move to sit
in it.

"We haven't talked in a long time. I haven't counted the years. Where's Henry J.?"

"He went to the snack bar to get me a Co' Cola and some chips. You boys bring anything to drink with you?"

"No," I said. "We didn't think about it."

I'd gotten one rig ready. I stood up and backed away from the water to make my cast. The line spun smoothly off the reel, and the bait landed noiselessly in the choppy water. The wind over the bay was so freighted with humidity that my own hair was going to be as curly as Big Al's if we stayed on Pelican Island for very long.

"Here," I said, handing the rod to Dino, who took it reluctantly, holding it out and away from his body as if it might infect him with the Ebola virus if it got too close.

"You do a lot of fishing, Dino," Big Al said. "I can tell."

Dino didn't answer. He just looked out at the line as if he were expecting a great white shark to take his hook and yank him into the bay.

Big Al watched Dino for a minute and then looked back over her shoulder.

"Here comes Henry J. now," she said. "If I'd known you boys were coming, I'd have had him get you a Co' Cola, too."

"Tru likes Big Red," Dino said.

Big Al shook her head at my bad taste as Henry J. arrived beside her chair. He was about six four, with the build of a retired linebacker who'd kept in shape. He was wearing a long-billed fishing cap, but I knew that underneath it he was completely bald, with a bumpy skull that a nineteenth-century phrenologist would have considered a prize trophy. He was wearing a T-shirt that was even tighter than Big Al's, and his had a different picture—a black revolver—and a different slogan—FIGHT CRIME. SHOOT BACK. His nose had been broken a lot. The bridge was as jagged as lightning. I was pretty sure he hadn't run into any doors.

He handed a paper cup and a bag of chips to Big Al and said, "What're these assholes doing here?"

I made a cast with my second rod, looked to the left and to the right, and said, "What assholes?"

"You never were very funny, Smith," he said. "No matter what you think. Ain't that what you say, Dino?"

There was a story that one of the breaks in Henry J.'s nose was a result of some old disagreement between him and Dino that had ended in a brief flurry of fisticuffs. It had happened when I was off the Island, though, and I didn't know the story. I'd never asked. I wasn't sure I wanted to know.

"I'm glad to see you, too, Henry J.," Dino said, still staring at his fishing line. "How's your nose?"

"You son of a bitch," Henry J. said. He thrust his cup at Big Al. "Hold this for me."

She didn't take the cup. "Calm down, Henry J. You don't want to go getting in a fight over some old grudge that you can't even remember. Not right here in public, anyway."

Henry J. didn't say a word. He just clamped his mouth on the straw in his cup and inhaled about half his drink.

After that, no one seemed inclined toward conversation. We all stared out at our lines, while the rest of the fishing contingent pretended to ignore us. Some of them were probably watching, though. When Big Al was around, lots of people were bound to be curious.

After maybe five minutes had gone by without a bite, I said, "I hear that you rent out beach houses for parties, Alice."

"You planning a party, Smith?" Henry J. asked.

I kept my eyes forward. "Maybe. If I can find a nice place to rent."

"I own a few beach houses," Big Al admitted. "People like to give me things."

In addition to her other enterprises, Big Al was reputed to lend money at interest rates that your local bank's chief loan officer would be arrested for just thinking about. Sometimes people couldn't pay back the loans, in which case Big Al was glad to take something valuable instead of the money, whether the owners wanted to give it up or not. After a visit from Henry J., they generally thought that giving up something valuable, like a beach house, for example, was a lot better than having their anatomy unpleasantly rearranged.

"Property isn't always an asset," I said. "Sometimes it can be a problem."

"How's that?" Big Al said.

"Renters, for one thing," I said. "Sometimes they tear things up, steal your fixtures, break things. It can be a real hassle. Or so I hear."

"Maybe you'd do something like that to the place where you're living, but not my renters. I don't allow that kind of thing."

"Those parties during spring break can get rowdy, though. Bad things can happen. Sometimes people get high and do things they'd never even think about under ordinary circumstances. Especially kids. They don't understand responsibility."

Big Al looked up at Henry J., who was still standing by her right shoulder. He bent down and set his cup by her chair.

"Not at my houses," Big Al said. "You know, the truth is, I don't like to be crowded when I fish. It's been nice to see you boys after all this time, and I've enjoyed talking to you. But I think you'd better move to a different spot now. The fish aren't biting here, anyway."

"If you need any help moving," Henry J. said, cracking his knuckles, "I'll give it to you."

I started reeling in my line, and Dino followed suit.

"We'll be going in a minute," I said. "It is a little crowded here, and as soon as Alice answers a couple of questions for me, Dino and I'll pack it in. I just want to know about a party at one of her beach houses."

"No questions," Henry J. said, lifting his hand and stepping closer to Dino, who spun around and slammed the butt of the heavy saltwater rod into Henry J.'s stomach as hard as he could.

He could have rammed the end of a matchstick into a brick wall for all the effect he had on Henry J., who didn't even move, didn't even take a deep breath. He just reached out, closed a big hand around the rod, and jerked it out of Dino's grip. Then he threw it in the bay.

"Hey," I said. "That wasn't Dino's rod. It was mine."

Henry J. looked about as concerned at my statement as he would have if I'd just told him that grass was green or water was wet. Dino's face was red, and I thought for just a fraction of a second that I was going to see whether he could break Henry J.'s nose a second time.

But it didn't work out that way. Henry J. just took a step forward and shoved Dino into the bay. Then he started for me.

It looked like I was going to get beaten to a pulp by myself after all.

12

I BENT OVER, grabbed the bait bucket, and stuck it out toward Henry J. "Here," I said. "Hold this."

He moved his hand to knock it aside, but I was too quick for him. I jerked the bucket back and threw saltwater and shrimp in his face.

That stopped him. He glared at me as he ran his hands over his face and then down his chest to swipe the water off his T-shirt. There was a shrimp on his shoulder, and he flicked it off into the bay with his finger. It was the lucky one. He crunched half the others under his size-twelve brogans as he came after me.

I decided that he was going to have to catch me before he killed me, and besides, I had a plan. Sort of. So I ducked under his reaching arms and scooted by Big Al's chair.

"You really should calm him down," I said in passing. "Think Prozac."

She stuck out a rock-hard hand to stop me, but I sidestepped past her, walking fast but not running. I was too proud to run.

Henry J. was right behind me, hot-footing it almost as fast as I was. People were staring at us openly now, but no one made a move to help me as I skedaddled down the walk. I looked back over my shoulder and saw Big Al getting ponderously out of her chair. Maybe all those overly developed muscles made rapid movement difficult.

I didn't see Dino anywhere, but I knew he would be all right. In fact, he was probably a lot better off than I was. We'd learned to swim almost as soon as we could walk, before we got too suave and sophisticated to spend any time in the surf, so he wouldn't drown. And no one was chasing him.

So he didn't have a problem, not unless Big Al conked him with a concrete block or something equally heavy. I didn't remember seeing anything like that lying around, and there were too many witnesses for Big Al to try something like that anyway. Being a criminal was one thing. Getting caught at it was something else again, and Big Al was too smart for that.

I was rapidly approaching the snack bar, which was actually a building with several levels, only one of which, the lower, was devoted to snacking.

I didn't think I had time for a snack, so I went up the wide staircase to the second level, skirting the side of the building on a balcony that had a great view of the bay if you were interested in that sort of thing, which I wasn't at the moment. I caught a glimpse of the Bolivar Peninsula and the metal lighthouse as I continued on my way.

Several people turned to see why I was in such a hurry. Their curiosity was satisfied when they saw Henry J. I could see it in their eyes. If he'd been hot on their trail, they'd have tried to keep well ahead of him, too. They turned back to their view of the ferryboats and the Gulf, feeling no need to get involved.

I didn't blame them a bit. I didn't particularly want to be involved, either, though I was about to get even more intimately in touch with Henry J. if things went as planned.

I'd been slowing down for the last few steps, letting Henry J. gain on me, and when I came to what I judged to be exactly the right spot, I stopped suddenly, turned, ducked, and threw my shoulder into Henry J.'s rocklike stomach just as he reached for me.

I didn't bend him much more than I could have bent an oak plank, but he was surprised, and when he grabbed for me I wasn't where he thought I'd be, so I managed to bend him just enough to allow me to straighten up and heave him over the balcony rail. He was no heavier than the small car that he might or might not have been named for.

He didn't have far to fall, only a few feet, before he thumped into the first-floor roof that sloped sharply down into some oleander bushes. There was one lonely white bloom still clinging to the branches among all the green leaves.

Henry J. flipped over on his stomach and tried to stop his slide down the roof, but there was nothing much to hold on to. His finger-nails made a really irritating sound as he tried to get a grip, but he probably didn't notice it. He had other things on his mind.

It would have been fun to stay around for a while and watch him thrashing around in the oleanders, but I thought I'd better go see about Dino. He didn't like being neglected for long periods of time.

I passed Big Al on my way back. She was moving at a leisurely pace, serene in the knowledge that Henry J. could put me down by using nothing more than his little finger. Or maybe the little finger and the thumb. She looked quite surprised to see that I was still able to walk, and when there was no sign of Henry J. at my back, she looked even more surprised. She even started moving a little faster. We passed, but she wasn't inclined to stop and chat. For that matter, neither was I.

When I got back to the spot where I'd left Dino, he was standing by Big Al's chair, drying his hair with a ragged towel someone had given him. The towel must have been used to wrap fish in. I could smell it from ten feet away.

Dino finished with the towel and handed it to an old man standing nearby. The man took it and grinned. He'd neglected to put his teeth in that morning, and he hadn't shaved in several days, but neither of those things seemed to bother him.

"Thanks for the towel," Dino said. "I appreciate it."

"Don't mention it," the man said. "I enjoyed seeing you hit that Henry J., even if you didn't knock him down. You're Dino, ain't you?"

"That's right."

Dino ran his fingers through his hair, trying to comb it down. For some reason I don't understand his hair is still nearly jet black, whereas I've had some gray in mine for years. Maybe I'm under more stress than he is.

"I remember your uncles," the old man told Dino. "They were real pistols. Brought movie stars to the Island all the time to be in those clubs of theirs. You remember those days?"

"Just barely," Dino said.

"It was somethin', lemme tell you. But it was a long time ago. What's the problem with you and Henry J.?"

"I don't have a problem with anybody," Dino said. He pointed to me. "He does."

"Who are you?" the old man asked me.

"Nobody," I told him. To Dino I said, "Are you ready to go?"

"I don't know. I'm sort of getting the hang of this fishing stuff. And the wind isn't quite freezing me. Why don't we stick around for a while, see if Big Al and Henry J. want to go eat at Gaido's later."

"Sarcasm doesn't become you," I said. "You've got the words, but you don't quite have the tune."

"I got your rod, though," he said, nudging it with his foot. "I figured that as long as I was down there, I might as well look for it."

"Great. Why don't we gather up my stuff and get out of here?"

He didn't argue. He grabbed the rods, and I got the tackle box and the now empty bait bucket.

"What happened to Henry J.?" he asked when we started back to my truck.

"He fell off the snack-bar balcony," I said.

"I'll bet he's not too happy about that."

"I didn't ask him. And if you'll hurry up, he won't have a chance to tell me."

We tossed the tackle in the truck bed and left the park. On the way back to Galveston we passed several people who had parked their cars by the road and were fishing from the shore.

"Cheapskates," Dino said. "They don't want to pay the admission fee."

"Maybe they like the fishing better here."

"Maybe. I guess you noticed that Big Al didn't much want to talk about any parties at her beach houses."

"I noticed," I said.

"What do you think that means?"

"I think it means that she knows something about what happened. I also think she's not going to tell me about it. Not yet anyway."

"Well," Dino said, "you learned that much at least. The trip wasn't completely wasted."

He was right. Big Al's behavior had given me plenty to think about. And that wasn't the only thing. But I wasn't ready to talk about the rest of it with Dino yet, because I wasn't exactly clear about it myself.

"I hope you're satisfied," he said.

"Why?"

"You dragged me out of my house, got me pushed in the bay, and humiliated me in front of a whole bunch of people, including an old guy with no teeth."

"I'm usually the one who gets wet when I'm working on a case," I said, thinking of a couple of recent instances, one of which had involved an alligator. That one hadn't been Dino's fault, however. I had to admit that much.

"You know what Sally Western said?" he asked.

"She said quite a few things. Which one in particular?"

"The one about me needing to get out more," he said.

"Oh, that. Yeah, I remember."

"Well, I have something for you to tell her for me the next time you see her."

"I'll tell her if I remember. What is it?"

Dino ran his fingers through his still damp hair and looked out the window at the tallow trees. Their leaves had all turned a deep orangy red, but most of them were still hanging on.

"Tell Sally that she was wrong," he said.

13

IT WAS NEARING sunset when we got back to Dino's. Half the western sky was the color of the tallow leaves.

Dino asked me if I wanted to come in for something to eat, but I was sure he was even less likely than I was to have anything edible in the house, so I turned him down. I would have suggested a restaurant, but he'd already had enough of being out of his house for one day. Besides, his clothes were still wet.

I drove home and parked in front. Nameless came running up to meet me at the door and charged inside ahead of me. I fed him, and sat in my recliner to look over my scanty notes and think things over.

The thinking didn't go so well at first, so I got up and put some CDs on the changer: a little Elvis, a little Kingston Trio (with Dave Guard, not the other guy), a little Everly Brothers, a little Drifters, a little Connie Francis. Eclectic, that's my middle name. I punched the Shuffle button and sat back down. Connie Francis launched into "Everybody's Somebody's Fool," and my mind started working better almost immediately.

There were lots of ifs involved in my thinking, but it seemed at least likely that there was some connection between the disappearance of Randall Kirbo and the death of Kelly Davis. Just what the connection was, I didn't know. But if they'd been seen together at a beach party, the possibility of a connection was strengthened. Too bad those two kids who'd seen them there had changed their stories.

I looked at my notes: Patrick Mullen and Travis Bittner. Room-mates at the University of North Texas. Patrick was from Texas City, only a few miles from where I was sitting. Travis was from Wichita Falls. I could imagine Patrick suggesting that they go to Galveston for spring break. They could have mooched food at Patrick's house for free and spent most of their days and nights on the beach.

I wondered if Patrick was home for Christmas vacation. If he was, I could stop by to see him on my way to talk to Chad Peavy, Randall's roomie, the one Tack Kirbo had insisted was probably lying. And he might have been, especially if he'd had a visit from Henry J., as Gerald Barnes suspected that Patrick and Travis had had.

Let's say the girl died at the party. Say that Randall Kirbo knew what had happened to her. Say that drugs were involved, not hard to imagine if Big Al were tossed into the mix. If all that were true, or close to true, it wasn't hard to imagine Henry J. intimidating, or even eliminating, witnesses.

Unlike Big Al, who as far as I knew had never even gotten a parking ticket, much less been arrested for something more serious, Henry J. had a rap sheet that any aspiring hard case would have envied. I knew for a fact that he'd been arrested for assault at least twice, and been questioned about an attempted murder. Rumor had it that more than once he'd done more than attempt it, though no one could prove it and no one was likely to talk on the record. Henry J. liked to use his hands, but he wasn't above using a knife. He didn't much like guns, however. They weren't personal enough.

Maybe I shouldn't have tossed him over the balcony. The Everly Brothers were singing "Problems." They didn't know what real problems were.

I wondered if Henry J. might pay *me* a visit. The thought was enough to make me get up and get my pistol out of the closet. It was a 7.65-millimeter Mauser in a sheepskin-lined case, but it wasn't loaded. In that condition, it wouldn't slow Henry J. down for a tenth of a second. I had to get the ammunition clips from a drawer in the kitchen. Gun safety is my middle name.

Nameless heard me open the drawer and thought I was probably getting him something to eat. After all, it had been practically a full hour since I'd fed him.

He looked up at me and said, "Mowr?"

I showed him the clip. "This isn't for you. Lead isn't good for cats. People either, for that matter."

"Mowr?"

"Forget it. Why don't you go outside and bully some lizards?"

"Mowr."

I took that for agreement, and walked to the door. Nameless followed me, but he took his time. He wasn't going to let me think I had the upper hand.

I opened the back door and he went through it at his own pace. Clouds had come in from out over the Gulf, and the night was very dark. I could hear the sound of the surf and the branches of the oleander bushes scraping against the side of the house.

I went back to the kitchen, oiled the Mauser, and shoved in one of the clips. Gun safety is fine, but I didn't want to take it to extremes. If Henry J. came around, I might need a pistol. Unlike him, I didn't believe that violence had to be intimate to be effective.

Before I sat back down in the recliner, I put the pistol on a little end table nearby where I could reach it easily. Then I listened to the Kingston Trio sing "A Worried Man." They didn't know the half of it.

I wondered just how Bob Lattner figured into things. Sure, he was supposedly investigating the disappearance of Randall Kirbo, but the Davis girl had been his niece. That gave him an emotional stake in things, and sometimes that interfered with professionalism. If he blamed Randall Kirbo for his niece's death, he might not care whether he ever got found.

After a while I picked up the collection of John O'Hara stories and started reading. Before long I'd forgotten about Henry J. and Big Al and even Randall Kirbo. But not Kelly Davis. For some reason she was always there, just at the back of my mind.

THERE ARE TWO schools of thought about interviewing people in connection with a crime or a suspected crime. You can either call them and ask permission to talk to them, or you can just drop by, cold, and see if they'll talk to you. I've tried it both ways, and I'm still not sure which one is best. This time I decided to do it the legit way and call ahead. That way had the advantage of saving time. I didn't want to drive all the way to Houston and then find out that Chad Peavy wasn't at home.

I waited until about nine o'clock the next morning to make my calls, figuring that people would either be staying in for the day or getting ready for church, and I got lucky with the first one.

Patrick Mullen's mother said that he was home and that he would be glad to talk to me. Of course, she might have said that because she somehow got the impression that I was representing his university's student retention office and that I wanted to talk to him about ways he might help us keep students in school if we gave him a part-time job.

Maybe I could smooth that over when I got to their house, or maybe not. I hoped it wouldn't matter because by the time they found out there had been a misunderstanding, I'd already be inside. It wouldn't be easy to get me out, not unless Patrick was bigger than Henry J.

Since my minor fabrication had worked so well with Mrs. Mullen, I was sorry I couldn't try it on the Peavys. Too bad the kid had dropped out of school. But then, a representative of the student retention office of Texas Tech University might very well be interested in interviewing a dropout to discover the reasons for his decision to leave.

Sure enough, Mr. Peavy found that a reasonable idea. He even sounded enthusiastic about it, which made me feel a little guilty, but not much. He thought my talk with his son might encourage him to return to classes, but I was pretty sure it would do just the opposite.

After I hung up the phone, I wondered if either Texas Tech or the University of North Texas actually had student retention offices. If they didn't, they were missing a bet. Maybe I should consider going straight. I could call up the universities and talk to someone about it. If they already had an office dedicated to retaining students, I could go to work for them, tracking down dropouts and counseling them.

Sure I could, about the same time that Big Al and Henry J. joined Big Brothers and Sisters.

I went to the bedroom to look for something to wear.

14

CONTRARY TO WHAT many people believe, I do own a sports coat, some slacks, a white shirt, a tie, and a regular pair of shoes. Of course the coat is about ten years out of style, and the tie is even older. As for the shoes, I have no idea whether anyone wears wing-tip loafers with tassels on them these days.

But no one expects academic types to be fancy dressers. They're supposed to be intellectuals, concerned with things of the mind, not with material possessions and outward show. Or at least that's what I hoped people expected.

What bothered me most was just how the S-10 fit into this scheme of things. I was pretty sure that even academic types wouldn't be driving to Texas City in a thirteen-year-old pickup truck. As a representative of the student retention office, I'd most likely have a school-issued car, some dull-colored four-door sedan. Since I didn't know anyone who owned a car like that, and since I didn't feel like renting one, I'd just have to take my chances.

I'd also have to hope that no one thought to ask me for a card. I didn't have a card of any kind. I did, however, have something almost as good: a clipboard with a yellow legal pad held down by the silver clamp at the top. A man carrying a clipboard and a yellow legal pad could hardly seem anything other than completely legitimate, especially if he was wearing a jacket and tie.

Tying the tie presented a problem, since I was considerably out

of practice, but I finally attained something resembling respect-
ability. The shirt could have used ironing, and the jacket didn't hang
exactly like an Armani original, but I'd shined the shoes, and the
crease in the slacks was above reproach.

"So," I said to Nameless, "how do I look?"

He looked up quizzically. "Mowr?"

"Not exactly the overwhelming endorsement I was hoping for, but
it'll do."

"Mowr?"

"Oh. You're right. I forgot the clipboard. No wonder you thought
something was lacking."

I got the clipboard and tucked it under my arm. "Well?"

"Mowr."

"I think so, too. They'll spill their guts to a sharp-looking guy like
me."

Nameless didn't even bother to respond to that one. He went off
somewhere to sleep, probably in my recliner, which I wouldn't ordi-
narily allow. He knew I was leaving, though, and he was going to take
advantage of the opportunity to misbehave. Cats are like that.

I DROVE INTO Texas City on Highway 146, going past the mile-long
stretch where the Union Carbide plant sprawled, a labyrinthine en-
tanglement of pipes and towers that always filled me with amazement.
I wasn't at all amazed at the myriad products the plant produced.
What amazed me was that anyone could ever have built something
so intricate and complicated in the first place.

Steam and smoke spiraled into the sky, and I resisted the urge to
hold my breath. I told myself I was only imagining that my throat was
beginning to tingle.

I turned down Palmer Highway and went toward town, if that was
the right word. Texas City is one of those towns that really isn't there
anymore. All the business had migrated out toward the interstate, and
I drove past huge discount houses and restaurants serving everything
you could think of, from Chinese food to barbecue.

Somewhere along the way, Palmer Highway changed names and
became Ninth Avenue. Fewer restaurants, but plenty of fast food:

sandwich shops, a Dairy Queen, a Jack in the Box. I didn't bother to stop to see if Mr. Box was there.

I drove between the high school and Moore Library. Not far ahead, on my right, a bulbous water tank with FIGHTING STINGAREES painted on it sat on top of its towering legs. I passed a park with a train engine and a caboose in it, and then I was nearing what had once been the downtown area. On both sides of the street were auto repair shops, car washes, pool supply houses, pest control offices.

The downtown itself was a mere shadow of its former self. There was a nicely restored building housing a coffee shop, and there was a pharmacy that looked prosperous, but that was about all. Down Sixth Street, the "Street of Memories" according to the sign, there was an old movie theater, the Showboat, with a poster for *Blackbeard the Pirate* displayed in front. Linda Darnell, Robert Newton, William Bendix. All of them dead now, like most of the downtown itself. Across from the theater was an entire block of deserted buildings, their plate-glass windows dark, some of them cracked, some of them covered with writing that said: GOING OUT OF BUSINESS.

I drove straight on down Ninth Avenue for a couple of blocks, into the residential area. The yards were full of tall palm trees and oaks that spread their branches all the way across the street. The houses were well kept but old, though not as old as the oak trees. There were other areas on the outskirts of town where the hundred-thousand-dollar houses were, but the Mullens didn't live there. I didn't blame them. The older homes had character, and they were only a few blocks from Bay Street and the Texas City Dike, a great place to fish. I wondered if Big Al ever went there, but I didn't think she did. She preferred Seawolf Park.

According to the directions I'd been given, the Mullen house was on the corner of Third Street and Thirteenth Avenue, and I found it easily. It was a big house of light-colored brick, with a wide front lawn, most of which was still green. In front of the house, as in front of a lot of others I'd passed, there were Christmas decorations standing under a palm tree. In some yards there had been scenes of Santa, with the reindeer pulling his sleigh, which looked pretty strange in their tropical setting, like the lights on the palms at the Galvez. But the Mullens had a manger scene, which somehow looked more appropriate. Not that I knew whether there were palm trees in Jerusalem. And if there were, they were probably a different kind of palm tree than the ones in Texas. Still, camels looked better standing under them than reindeer did, at least to me.

I parked the truck on the side street, hoping that no one in the house would notice it, and walked around to the front yard. My knock on the door was answered by a short woman with big hair and a wide smile.

"Mr. Smith?" she said.

I admitted that I was, holding my clipboard in front of me so she couldn't miss it.

"Come right on in," she said. "I'm Carolyn Mullen. Patrick's in his room."

I followed her down a short hall, through the living room, and into another hall, where she stopped and knocked on the second door.

"Patrick?" she said. "Mr. Smith from the college is here to see you."

A voice behind the door said, "Come on in," and Carolyn Mullen turned the knob.

When the door opened, I looked over her shoulder and saw that Patrick kept the place pretty neat. There was a poster of the UNT basketball team on one wall and one of Cindy Crawford on another. The bed was made up, and Patrick was sitting in the only chair in the room, which was at a small desk. He was looking at what might have been a chemistry book.

He closed the book, then got up and crossed over to us. His mother stepped back and to the side, and I put out my hand.

"Hi, Patrick," I said. "I'm Truman Smith, from the student retention office."

He shook my hand briefly, then dropped it. "Yeah. That's what Mom said. You want to talk to me about something?"

"About keeping students in college," I said, waggling my clipboard. When you have a prop, use it, I always say.

"You two are welcome to use the living room if you want to," Mrs. Mullen said. "I'll be in the kitchen."

She left us there, looking at one another.

"Let's go in the living room," Patrick said. "I don't have any chairs in here."

We went back to the living room. There was an artificial Christmas tree with blinking lights in one corner, but there weren't many presents under it. The carpet was almost new, thick, and much too light-colored for my taste. The chairs, the couch, and the coffee table were older. Patrick sat in one of the chairs and made himself comfortable. I sat on the couch, got out my pen, balanced my clipboard on my knee, and wrote his name on the legal pad.

"So," he said. "What's this about a job?"

He was a good-looking kid, not much taller than his mother, with wide-set, intelligent eyes and longish hair that fell artfully over his ears.

"We need help," I said. "Every semester, all through the semester, colleges lose students. They withdraw from their classes and disappear, and most of the time we don't even know why. We're trying to get in touch with them, find out why they left, and see if there's something we can do to get them back. We need all the students we can get, since our funding is based on them."

"Yeah, I know about that," he said, "and I could use the job. Mom doesn't make a lot of money as a secretary at the plant. But what would I have to do?"

One of the reasons I like working at home with my computer is that I rarely have to lie to anyone, and I didn't want to lie to Patrick Mullen. But I reminded myself that he'd probably lied to the police about things, and was therefore just as guilty of lying as I was. Maybe two wrongs don't make a right, but the fact that the first wrong wasn't mine made me feel a little better about things.

So I said, "You'd make some phone calls, talk to people, ask a few questions. That's really all there is to it. Of course, you'd have to record their answers on a form we'd provide, but I'm sure you could handle all that."

"I think so. It doesn't sound so hard. Who recommended me? Was it Professor Williams?"

"Let me see." I flipped through a few pages of my legal pad, then looked up at him. "Did you say Williams?"

"He teaches in the management department. I made an A in his class last semester, and he told me I was one of the best students he'd had in a while. I thought maybe he recommended me."

"Oh, yes," I said, putting my finger on a page. "Here it is. Professor Williams, management department. He's the one, all right."

"I figured. So how many hours a week would I be working?"

I heard pots rattle in the kitchen, and I thought about how tough it must be for a single mother to be sending a kid to college. I wished that the job offer were real.

"Just a few," I said, tired of the game. "What you'd do is call up the students on a list that the office provided. I have a sample list and questionnaire right here."

I took them from behind my legal pad. I'd printed them out on my computer before I left, hoping the questionnaire looked somewhat legitimate. As for the names and phone numbers, I'd made them all up, except for the first two.

He didn't even look at the questionnaire because he saw the two names first: Kelly Davis and Randall Kirbo.

15

HIS EYES WIDENED, then narrowed as he looked up from the paper that he still held.

"You're not from the school," he said, keeping his voice low so his mother couldn't hear. "I bet you never heard of Dr. Williams."

He had me there. I didn't know Dr. Williams from Dr. Seuss. So I said, "That's right. I'm here for a different reason. I want to know about two names on that list I gave you. The first two."

"I ought to throw you out of here."

I have to admit that he had spirit. I was nearly a foot taller than he was and in pretty good shape for someone he probably thought of as an old guy.

"You don't want to do that," I said. "We could damage the furniture. Besides, it might embarrass your mother."

He looked toward the kitchen, where the sounds of meal preparation continued. Then he looked back at me. He didn't seem pleased to see that I was still there. Maybe he'd thought I'd take the opportunity to slip away quietly to avoid a thrashing.

"You got in here under false pretenses," he said.

"I'm sorry about that," I said, trying to sound as if I meant it. "But I had to talk to you."

"You're not a cop, then. I've already talked to them."

"No, I'm not a cop."

"If you're not a cop, then I don't have to tell you a thing."

"That's true. You don't. But Kelly Davis is dead and Randall Kirbo is missing. It seems to me that you'd want to do something about that."

"I don't even know who they are," he said. "Why should I want to do anything about them?"

"Well, you see, that's where I just don't believe you," I told him. "I think you did know them, or at least you saw them at a party you went to. That's what you told the police when you talked to them."

He shook his head. "I was wrong, though. The pictures the cops had weren't very good, and I made a mistake. Haven't you ever made a mistake?"

There were beads of sweat on his forehead, but the house wasn't all that warm. He'd made a mistake, all right, but not about identifying the pictures.

"It's going to be easy enough for me to find out if you're telling the truth," I said. "There's another witness, someone who saw you there at the party."

"He changed his mind, too."

"How do you know?"

"I just know, that's all." His voice was rising, and his face was turning red. "And that's all I'm going to say about it. You can get out of here now."

The kitchen got very quiet.

"Patrick?" his mother called.

It was time for me to go. I stood up and tucked my clipboard under my arm.

Mrs. Mullen walked into the room and looked at her son, who was still sitting in the chair, gripping its arms as if he might be trying to crush them.

"Is something wrong?" she asked.

"Everything's fine," I said. "I was just leaving. Patrick's going to come by my office when he gets back to school and have a talk about that job."

Mrs. Mullen smiled uncertainly and looked at her son, who didn't look a lot like someone who'd just been offered lucrative employment.

"That's nice," she said. "I suppose."

"He'll be an asset to the school," I said, backing toward the door. "I'm glad Dr. Williams recommended him."

Patrick's eyes were wide with disbelief, as if he couldn't believe that I'd dare to lie so blatantly. I wanted to tell him that if he could do it, so could I, but it didn't seem to be the right time to try imparting a moral lesson.

"We're having roast for lunch, if you'd like to stay," Mrs. Mullen said to me.

"I'd love to, but I have an appointment in Houston. I'm going to be a little late as it is. Thanks for the invitation, though."

"You're welcome. Thank you for coming by."

"My pleasure."

I was at the door, and I opened it. Mrs. Mullen was looking at Patrick as if hoping he would say something nice to me to solidify his chance of getting the job.

He didn't say a word. He was still glaring at me when I closed the door, and I wondered how he'd explain his behavior to his mother. Or if he'd even bother to try.

I DROVE PAST the muffler shops and transmission shops, then out past the discount stores. I crossed Highway 146 and headed for Interstate 45, passing the community college and a huge shopping mall.

As I turned onto the interstate, I could see Gulf Greyhound Park on my left. I thought about stopping to put down a few bets on the dogs, but I didn't have time. I had to talk to Chad Peavy and see what his reaction to my visit would be. I hoped I could get more out of him than I'd managed with Patrick Mullen.

As I drove toward Dickinson, a town that had once been nearly as wide-open as Galveston, I thought about what I'd learned from my short visit to Texas City.

For one thing, it was clear that Patrick knew a lot more than he was willing to tell, but now I wondered if his forgetfulness was entirely due to a visit from Henry J. It was hard to judge whether he was afraid because of what Henry J. might do to him or for some other reason.

What other reason? Could Patrick Mullen have been something more than just a witness to the fact that Randall Kirbo and Kelly Davis had been at the same party? Could he have had something to do with the girl's death? Judging from the look on his face as I left his house, and from the grip he had on those chair arms, he was capable of violence under the right circumstances—or the wrong ones. Nearly everyone is.

I wasn't sure about anything that might have happened at the party, but I didn't think that Mullen was going to break down and change his story just to get things off his chest. It was going to take more than just a casual attempt to get anything out of him. I'd left his house quietly, but that didn't mean I wouldn't be talking to him again if I could just figure out what it was that I wanted to say.

I flicked on the truck's radio and picked up the Beatles doing "I'm Down." They weren't the only ones.

I PASSED DICKINSON and then League City. I was getting close to the Clear Lake area when I noticed that I was being followed.

Or I thought I was. There's so much traffic on the interstate that it's not always easy to tell. However, I was driving the legal speed limit, seventy miles an hour, which made me an exception. I was in the middle lane, and cars were zipping by me on both the right and left. Now and then the drivers would give me a look of annoyance, as if I were some kind of idiot for getting in their way. The fact that someone was going even slower than I was and hanging back about a quarter of a mile was enough to make me suspicious, especially since it was a black Cadillac Seville, the kind of car that Big Al owned and that Henry J. frequently drove for her.

Of course there are quite a few black Cadillac Sevilles in the Houston area, and I was probably worrying about nothing. I slowed down to find out.

The Cadillac slowed down, too.

I sped up to eighty, which wasn't really pushing the S-10's six-cylinder engine and which put me at about the same speed as most everyone else. I even passed a couple of people.

The Cadillac kept pace, which might not have meant anything at all. Or it might have meant that I was right about Henry J. being on my tail.

There were a number of ways of handling things. I could have pulled over to the side of the road to see if the Cadillac would continue on its merry way. If it did, I might get a look at the driver, though I could tell even from a distance that the windows were tinted darker than legally allowable, just like the windows on Big Al's car.

Or I could have tried some movie stunt, like somehow letting the Cadillac catch up with me and then forcing it off the road by bumping into its side and running up a big bill at some body shop.

I didn't think my insurance would cover any stunt like that, however, even if I survived it, so I decided to see if I could lose whoever it was. After all, I knew where I was going, and he didn't.

At least I thought he didn't. I wouldn't have put it past Big Al to have put a tap on my phone or to have stationed Henry J. near my house with some kind of sophisticated listening device that would pick up every word I spoke.

We'd see. When I got to Houston, I'd put the moves on him. I was fairly sure I could shake him, and if he turned up later on, then I'd know he had inside information.

If he didn't turn up, Big Al would probably do something terrible to him.

Which was just fine with me.

16

IT WAS EVEN easier than I'd thought it would be. I got onto Loop 610, then drove around it until I came to Highway 288. From 288 I took the exit for the Medical Center, with its maze of hospitals and parking lots. I didn't spend much time in that area, but I figured that Henry J. didn't, either. It was just a matter of getting a little lead on him and hiding the truck from sight.

When I took the exit, the Cadillac tried to make up some of the distance between us, but it was already too late. I made a few zigs and a few zags and even got lost myself. I went into and out of a couple of parking lots and finally pulled into a spot between two custom vans that towered over my little truck like a couple of semis.

I sat there for ten minutes, listening to the radio recycling the same old oldies and wishing I'd brought the O'Hara book with me to read. There was no sign of the Cadillac in that time, so I pulled back out onto the street and headed toward West University, better known as West U, a community not far from the Rice campus, where all the streets were named for famous literary figures. If you've ever yearned for a classy address on a street named for Shakespeare or one of the Romantic poets, then West U is the place for you.

As it happened, the Peavys lived on Coleridge, whose name always reminded me of "The Rime of the Ancient Mariner," portions of which, for some reason I'd never tried to figure out, had been stuck in my memory ever since my eighth-grade English class with Mrs.

Morgan. As far as I could tell, the verses had never served a useful purpose in my life. After all, what possible good was it that I remembered the two lines that said, "Yea, slimy things did crawl with legs upon the slimy sea"? I was sure Mrs. Morgan would have been proud of me for recalling it, though.

The Peavy house was white and two stories tall. There was a large boat covered with canvas parked in front of a black BMW in the driveway. The Christmas decorations were limited to a tasteful handmade wreath on the front door, where I was met by all the Peavys, who seemed quite happy to see me. Obviously, they hadn't been talking to the Mullens within the last hour or so.

Chad's parents were dressed casually but expensively, all natural fabrics, of course, whereas Chad was wearing a pair of old jeans and a flannel shirt that might have come from Wal-Mart. He was big, bigger than I was, and a lot wider through the shoulders. Shaking hands with him was like shaking a hand carved from a block of wood.

"I hope you'll be able to talk some sense into Chad," Mr. Peavy said as he led the way to the den, a room with a big-screen TV, a sectional sofa, and several chairs. There was also a Christmas tree, a fir of some kind, not artificial, about seven feet high. There were plenty of gifts under it, wrapped in red and green paper.

"Chad just seems to have lost interest in school," Mr. Peavy said. "I don't know why."

"That's why I'm here," I said, giving them a quick look at my clipboard and pad. "My job is to try to get him to come back. We don't like to lose any students, of course, but your son is a special case."

"We've always felt that way, too," Mrs. Peavy said. She was a cheerful-looking woman with hair so black that I was certain it was dyed. "He could do so well if he'd just try."

"Not to mention that he could help out the football team," I said, getting into the spirit of things.

"That's the truth," Mr. Peavy said. "He could have been really good if he'd just put his mind to it. I think the disappearance of his roommate just took the fun out of things for him."

The three of us chattered on that way for a few seconds, while Chad stood awkwardly to one side and said absolutely nothing. It was obvious that meeting with me hadn't been his idea.

"Why don't the two of you leave Chad and me alone for a while?" I suggested to the Peavys. "Sometimes these interviews are a little awkward if the parents are in the room."

Mr. Peavy said that he understood completely, and he and his wife disappeared.

"We might as well sit down," I said to Chad when they were gone.

Chad sat in a chair, folded his arms across his chest, and looked at me. He still hadn't said anything.

I looked at my clipboard, ran my finger down the legal pad, and said, "Let's see. Your roommate was Randall Kirbo, is that right?"

"Yeah," Chad said.

"He's another student we'd like to have back. I understand that there's some problem there, however."

"Yeah."

I pretended to refer to the legal pad again. "He didn't come back to school after spring break. Neither did you. Any connection?"

"Nah."

"Your major was communications, right, Chad?"

"Huh?"

"Just a little joke." I smiled to show him that I was only kidding around, then looked back at the legal pad. "It says here that Randall was at some kind of party and that he was never seen again after that. You were there, too, isn't that right?"

Chad leaned against the back of his chair as if trying to get as far away from me as possible.

"What's this got to do with student retention?" he asked.

It was nice to find out that he could string several words together at the same time.

"Well, Chad, as you know, I'm interested in helping the college retain students. If we can find out why they left in the first place, we might be able to persuade them to come back and continue their educations. If something happened at that party to cause two of our students to decide to leave college forever, then we'd like to know about it. You see?"

"No."

Talking to Chad was a little like talking to Nameless, though I was beginning to wonder if Nameless didn't have a slightly larger vocabulary.

I tried again. "Let me put it this way, Chad. If we could find out what happened at that party, we might be able to get in touch with Randall and talk to him the way I'm talking to you."

Chad just looked at me. Subtlety wasn't going to get me anywhere with him.

"I don't seem to be getting through to you, Chad," I said. "So I'm going to level with you. I don't care about you at all. The coach told me that you were a lousy football player and that he didn't care whether you came back or not. But he wants me to find out about Randall. He says Randall could be all-conference next year."

"He's fulla shit, then," Chad said.

I had to give Chad credit for one thing; he was making it easy for me to lie to him.

"Maybe so," I said. "Now, about that party. There was a girl named Kelly there."

Chad uncrossed his arms, then recrossed them even more tightly in front of him than before.

"Who said there was?" he asked. "Who said there was any party? I didn't go to any party."

"A young man named Patrick Mullen says you did. He lives down in Texas City."

"I never heard of him. He didn't tell you anything about any party, or any Kelly, either."

"Well, that's where you're wrong, Chad. He told me quite a bit about her. He told me that Randall went to a party with her at a beach house, and that he saw you there, too. He said there was a lot of drinking going on, and that sometime during the evening Kelly and Randall went off by themselves. He didn't see them after that, but you did."

"That's a damn lie. He didn't tell you all that."

It was a damned lie, all right, but I certainly wasn't going to admit it.

"Sure he told me," I said. "Why wouldn't he?"

"Because he'd better not have, that's why." Chad was sweating even more than Patrick had been. "He knows better than to say something like that."

"Why? Is he afraid of Henry J.?"

Chad looked puzzled. It was a look that came so naturally to him that I couldn't tell whether he was faking it or not.

"Henry who?"

"Don't kid with me, Chad. You know exactly who I'm talking about."

"No, I don't. You're talking crazy, about parties and stuff that I don't know anything about. And I don't think you're here from any student retention office, either."

Chad wasn't exactly quick on the uptake, but he'd eventually found me out. I decided to reward him by telling him the truth, or part of it.

"You catch on fast, Chad," I said. A little flattery might not hurt. "I'm actually a private detective. I've been hired by Randall's parents to find out what happened to him."

"I don't know what happened to him. I don't know about any party or any girl named Kelly Davis."

"Who said her name was Davis?" I asked.

Chad looked panicked. "You did."

"I don't think so, Chad. I left that little detail out."

"Then the cops must've mentioned her. I went over all that stuff about Randall with the cops a long time ago."

"But you didn't tell them the truth. You lied to them about not knowing what happened to Randall. You know he disappeared after that party."

Chad wiped his forehead with one of his hard hands, then wiped his hand across the leg of his jeans.

"I don't know what you're talking about. I was never at any party. I don't know if Randall was, either. And I don't know anything about this Kelly person."

Chad was talking a little more, but he wasn't helping me. He was as stubborn as his hand was hard. Maybe a few more lies would crack him.

"There was someone else at the party," I said. "Someone who came forward just last week and talked to the police in Galveston. So you might as well tell me what happened. I already know most of it."

Chad's mouth twisted. "That bitch."

"Which bitch are you talking about?"

"You know which one. That damn Sharon. I knew she couldn't keep quiet."

I felt for just a second as if someone had sucker-punched me in the solar plexus, but I tried not to show it. There were probably hundreds of girls named Sharon in Galveston. This one didn't have to be the one I was thinking of, though if she were, it would explain something that had been bothering me.

"Blondish hair?" I said. "Blue eyes? Tall?"

"Yeah, yeah. That's her."

I asked him what her last name was.

"Matthews, I think. I don't remember."

I'd been afraid he was going to say that.

"I shoulda known she'd talk sooner or later," he said.

I took a deep breath. "She did. So why don't you?"

Chad slumped in his chair and looked at his feet.

"OK," he said. "I'll tell you."

17

SOMETIMES I'M NOT nearly as clever as I think I am, and this was one of those times. I hadn't lost Henry J. at all. He was waiting for me when I came out of the house.

The Cadillac Seville was parked around the corner, right in front of my truck. Henry J. was leaning against the side of the S-10, picking his teeth and looking up at a squirrel in one of the oak trees. When he saw me, he lost interest in the squirrel. He grinned at me, snapped the toothpick in two, and threw it on the street.

"There's a pretty stiff fine for littering in West U," I told him.

"Yeah? I wish you hadn't told me that. Now I'm scared half to death."

He didn't look scared at all. He actually looked quite happy to see me.

"You should be scared," I said. "The cops here don't like litterbugs."

His grin got wider. "Guess I'll have to mop up the street, then. With you."

I'd spent the night with my Mauser beside the bed, but I hadn't thought to bring it with me. Even if I'd brought it, it would have been inside the truck where I couldn't get to it. I wondered if I could convince Henry J. that my clipboard was a lethal weapon. I didn't really think so.

In fact, I hadn't really been thinking at all. If I had been, I would have realized that Henry J. didn't have to follow me. He would have guessed that if I'd visited Patrick Mullen, the next logical stop would be at Chad Peavy's house, and he obviously had the address. He'd probably been there before.

"The cops are pretty tough in West U," I said. "You wouldn't want to start something that might get both of us thrown in jail."

Today, Henry J. was wearing a T-shirt that showed a target silhouette with a red bull's-eye on it. A black hole was in the center of the bull's-eye, and printed above and below the silhouette was GUN CONTROL MEANS HITTING YOUR TARGET. Matched automatic pistols in holsters dangled from the "u" in "Gun" and the "o" in "Control."

Henry J. wasn't wearing a pistol, though. Not that I could see. And I would have seen it if he'd been wearing one. His jeans and T-shirt were skintight. I was sure he didn't think he'd need a gun for me.

He started toward me, still grinning, completely relaxed, light on his feet, his hands swinging loosely at his sides, ready to snap me in two just like he'd done the toothpick. He knew I wasn't going to get away from him this time.

His problem was that he wasn't a fast learner. He should have known from his experience in Seawolf Park that I was a tricky son of a gun.

I pressed the clasp on the clipboard, and the legal pad fell to the sidewalk.

"You dropped something, Smith," Henry J. said. "Or did you just piss your pants?"

"Damn," I said. "Those are my notes. I gotta have those."

I bent slightly forward as if I were going to pick up the pad, and in the same motion I flung the clipboard toward Henry J. as hard as I could. It flew at him like some kind of deformed Frisbee.

Henry J. was the kind of guy who, given the opportunity, could probably catch flies out of midair with his bare hands. But he'd been distracted by the thought that I might have some important notes, which Big Al would certainly want to see, and his eyes were on them.

So he didn't quite see the clipboard coming at him in time to do anything about it. Its edge cracked against the bridge of his nose with a sound like a tree branch breaking. His nose hadn't been beautiful before. It was going to look a lot worse now.

Henry J. screamed and dropped to his knees. His hands went to his face, and I could see blood running between his fingers as I stepped by him.

"You can have the notes," I told him as I got in the truck. "The clipboard, too."

I don't think he heard me, though.

I LEFT WEST U by way of Bissonett Street. At Kirby I drove by a store with a giant shoe rotating above it. Just beyond it I passed a store called Murder by the Book, and before long I was at the Museum of Fine Arts, then the colorful Children's Museum, and then at the edge of the medical center. When I came to Highway 288, I crossed over, turned left, and headed for the interstate.

I looked in the rearview mirror, but there was no sign of the Cadillac Seville. I wasn't surprised. I didn't think Henry J. would be up to driving for a while. For all I knew he was still kneeling on the sidewalk, feeling his nose.

Henry J. had never liked me, and I had a feeling that the events of the last couple of days weren't going to elevate me in his esteem. I wasn't going to worry about it, however. I had too many other things on my mind.

Like Chad Peavy, who had admitted to being at the party that Randall Kirbo and Kelly Davis had attended, as I'd guessed he had been. He'd eventually told me most of what he knew about what went on there. Unfortunately, he didn't know as much as I'd hoped, or pretended that he didn't.

He did tell me where the beach house was, however, so I could probably confirm whether it belonged to Big Al, not that I had any doubts.

He also admitted that he'd seen Davis and Kirbo together there. They hadn't been together at the beginning, because Chad and Randall had gone in Chad's car.

And Chad had stopped short of saying that his earlier memory lapses had come about because he'd been threatened by Henry J. I wondered if Henry J. would be paying him a little visit that afternoon. It didn't seem likely, considering the condition of Henry J.'s nose.

According to Chad, there had been plenty of drinking at the party, as I'd suspected, and a few drugs other than alcohol had been ingested, though not, of course, by him.

"There was some Ecstasy," he said, "and some other stuff. I don't mess with those things."

I didn't really believe him, but I didn't think it mattered what he'd done. I wanted to know about Davis and Kirbo. And that's what he couldn't tell me.

"They weren't there long," he said. "They must've left. Or if they were there, they went upstairs. I don't know what was going on up there."

"Sure you do, Chad."

"Nope. I was downstairs the whole time. I don't have any idea about the upstairs. I don't even know if they went up there."

Somehow I didn't believe a word of it. Both Chad Peavy and Patrick Mullen knew more than they were telling, and I was afraid that Henry J. was the reason. I would have been afraid of him, too, if I'd still been a college kid. For that matter, I *was* afraid of him, and I was long past my college days.

The S-10 sailed down the interstate, taking me back past League City, Dickinson, and Texas City. The traffic on my side of the highway wasn't bad, but I was glad I wasn't on the other side, which was three lanes of bumper-to-bumper automobiles, all of them tourists who had spent a day at Dickens on the Strand, and all of them now on their way back home. Their average speed was probably around fifty-five, which must have been torture for most of them. I cruised along at a steady seventy, thinking.

When I wasn't thinking about Chad Peavy and Patrick Mullen, I was thinking about Dino, my old buddy Dino, my childhood pal, and about what I was going to do to him when I saw him. I still hadn't quite made up my mind when I stopped the truck in front of his house.

It was a good thing I'd left the Mauser at home, though. If I'd had it with me, I might have shot him.

18

DINO OPENED HIS door and I shoved past him and into his living room.

"You're looking spiffy, Tru," he called after me. "What's the occasion?"

When I didn't answer, he followed me in and said, "Hey, Tru, what's the matter?"

"You," I said. "You're the matter."

The giant television set was playing some infomercial in which an incredibly irritating young man with a long ponytail was screaming about the wonders of some weird piece of exercise equipment. Dino went to the coffee table and touched a button on the remote control. The ponytail disappeared as the TV screen went black. I was grateful for that, at least.

"What do you mean *I'm* the matter?" Dino asked. "What are you talking about?"

"You know damned well what I'm talking about. I'm talking about you hitting Henry J. in the gut with my fishing rod yesterday."

Dino laughed, which just made me angrier. I could feel my face getting red, but Dino didn't notice.

"I didn't break your rod, did I?" he asked.

"No. That's not the problem."

"Then what is?"

"You know what it is."

Dino sat down. "You keep saying that, but I really don't have any idea." He looked up at me. "Don't just stand there like a store dummy. Why don't you have a seat?"

"I don't want to have a seat."

"I guess you don't. Would a Big Red help?"

"Not this time," I said.

"Must be really serious, then."

"It's serious, all right. You've lied to me right from the start. I expect clients to lie to me when I'm working on a case, Dino, but you aren't my client. You're my friend. You're supposed to tell me the truth."

"Shit," Dino said.

"I want you to tell me what's going on, and I want you to tell me right now. Otherwise, I'm leaving, and you can tell the Kirbos I'm sorry, but I won't be looking for their kid any longer."

"Listen, Tru, it's not like you think."

"That's what people always tell me, but usually they're lying then, too."

"Look, I'm going in the kitchen and getting you a Big Red. I bought some special, just in case you came by, so you might as well drink one. I even put the cans in the refrigerator so they'd be cold. I know you'd rather drink out of the can than pour Big Red over ice."

I gave him a mature and reasoned response: "I don't want any of your damned Big Red."

"It's not mine. I bought it for you. So sit down while I get it."

He stood up, and left the room. I fumed for a few seconds and then sat down. I'd drink his Big Red, but I wasn't letting him off the hook.

It was Chad Peavy who'd clued me in. I'd wondered why Dino had slammed Henry J. with his fishing rod. There hadn't seemed to be a reason for it, and I probably should have asked about it after it happened. When Chad told me that Sharon Matthews was at the party, I knew the answer.

Sharon was Dino's daughter. She had lived with her mother, Evelyn, a former prostitute who was now completely respectable, and Dino had hardly known Sharon until she'd disappeared one day a year or so back. I'd located her for him, and now their relationship was improving, just as Dino's relationship with Evelyn was improving. Evelyn was better at getting him out of the house than I was, and

I hoped that eventually the two of them would decide to live together, maybe even get married.

Sharon had been attending the local community college, and from what Dino had told me, she was doing very well. She was supposed to graduate that summer with her associate's degree and go on to the University of Houston to get a teaching certificate. It was hard for Dino to believe that someone related to him was going to be a teacher. It seemed too respectable, somehow.

Apparently, Sharon wasn't so respectable that she was above going to a spring break party in one of Big Al's beach houses, however.

Dino came back in the room and handed me the can of Big Red. He'd wrapped a paper napkin around it, but I could feel the cold of the can even through the paper.

He sat back down and watched me take a sip of the drink.

"I didn't put any poison in it, if that's what you're thinking," he said.

"I wasn't thinking that. But I wouldn't put it past you."

"Look, Tru, I never lied to you. I just left out a few things."

"Just little things, though," I said. "Things anybody might overlook. Like a dead body."

"Maybe I should start at the beginning and tell you the whole thing."

"What a unique idea. Why didn't I think of that?"

"You know what you said to me yesterday?" he asked. "About sarcasm?"

"I remember."

"Well, it doesn't become you, either."

"I can't help it. I'm pissed off."

"I don't blame you. It's my fault. I admit it. No wonder you don't trust me."

"Oh, I trust you all right. I trust you to lie like a rug."

"That's a pretty good one. Did you think it up right on the spur of the moment?"

I took a drink of Big Red and set the can on his coffee table.

"I thought you were going to tell me the truth," I said. "From the beginning."

"Yeah, I guess I was." He stared at something just above my head for a while. "It's hard to know where to start."

"At the beginning. Like you said."

"I'm not sure what the beginning is."

"The party," I told him. "Start with the party. I'd really like to hear about that party. And try to tell the truth. I'm going to check it with Sharon."

"I wish you could leave her out of it, Tru. She's had a tough time, and this isn't going to help her any."

"Maybe not. But she's in it already. Now tell me about the party."

"All right," he said.

SHARON HAD FOUND out about the party the way kids do, through hearing about it from someone who'd heard about it from someone else. She didn't have anything else to do that evening, and she thought it might be fun. She'd been working on a term paper that was due in her English class the day after spring break ended, and she'd thought the party would be a good way to relax for a while.

"She didn't know very many people who were there," Dino said. "Just a couple of kids from the college. She didn't know Kelly Davis or Randall Kirbo at all. They were there, though. She remembers hearing the names. There was another kid there who comes into this, too."

I thought I knew who that someone was. Chad Peavy. But I let that pass. I'd ask Sharon.

"Sharon didn't think anything else about them, though," Dino went on. "Not until she saw the picture of Kelly Davis in the paper."

"But she didn't go to the police," I said.

"My family doesn't go to the police," Dino said, which was true.

It didn't matter that Dino wasn't involved in anything illegal and that he never had been, at least not directly. It didn't matter that his uncles had been dead for years and that during most of that time Galveston had been as tame as an afternoon social at a Baptist church.

It didn't even matter that his daughter might know something that would help the police in their investigation into Kelly Davis's death. Dino and his family didn't go to the police under any circumstances. He didn't even like it that I occasionally helped out the police, or that they helped me out.

None of that mattered. What mattered was the time-honored family policy: no cops.

"OK," I said. "She didn't go to the police. But I'm not the police. The least you could have done was tell me the situation."

Dino shook his head. "I didn't know the situation. When Tack called me and asked me if I could help him out, I didn't know that his son had anything to do with that party. I didn't know until yesterday, when you started talking to Big Al. When you said you wanted to ask about a party at one of her beach houses, it was like everything just connected right there in my head. So I clobbered Henry J. before we got to that part of it. It was just a gut reaction."

I had to smile, thinking about it. "And he shoved you in the bay."

"Yeah, but you got him back for me."

"You should see him today. I got him again."

"You did? How?"

"I'll tell you later. Maybe. I want to know more about that party."

Sharon had hung around the party with the young man she'd met, probably Chad Peavy, but she hadn't enjoyed herself. There was too much drinking. Too many drugs.

"Sharon doesn't go for that kind of stuff," Dino said. "Sure, she drinks now and then, maybe a glass of wine, but nothing heavy. And no drugs, not ever."

Dino was insistent on that last point, and it was a point of honor that his uncles had never been involved in the drug business. Gambling, yes. Illegal liquor, sure. Prostitution, no question. But not drugs. Never that.

"Have you talked to her since yesterday?" I asked.

"Yeah. I called her right after you brought me home."

"But you didn't call me to tell me any of this."

"Yeah. I know I should have, but I thought maybe you could figure things out without having to talk to her."

I picked up my Big Red and took a couple of long swallows. I set the can back down and said, "Well, you thought wrong. Let's go."

"Go where?"

"To see your daughter," I said.

19

SHARON LIVED IN a small apartment on the top floor of an old house only a couple of blocks from the Galvez Hotel, down toward Broadway. It was getting late, and paying her a visit meant that we might be out after dark, so Dino wasn't keen on the idea. He didn't like going out at all if he didn't have to, and he liked going out at night even less.

"It won't kill you," I told him. "I'll even treat you to supper."

He looked longingly at his TV set. "I don't want supper," he said.

"Look," I said, "I don't much care what you want. This is all your fault, and you're coming with me, whether you like it or not."

His mouth hardened. "I'm not sure you could make me go if I didn't want to."

"Jesus Christ, Dino, you really crack me up. You got me into this mess in the first place, and since then you've lied to me and held out on me. Now you want to pull some macho tough-guy crap with me instead of just coming along to help me talk to your daughter. OK. How do you want to handle it? Draw a line on the floor and dare me to step across it?"

"You make it sound pretty silly when you put it that way."

"It is pretty silly. We're grown-ups, after all."

Considering what my earlier feelings and actions had been, I was now being a genuine hypocrite. But you do what you have to do.

"Yeah, I guess you're right," Dino said. "Let me call Sharon and tell her we're coming over."

"Let's just surprise her," I said.

"What if she's not there?"

"Then we'll go see her mother. I want to talk to her, too."

"You really know how to show a guy a good time," Dino said.

FINDING OUT THAT her mother had been a prostitute had been quite a shock for Sharon, and one result had been the disappearance that had caused Dino so much concern. But that wasn't why she was living alone now. She and Evelyn had pretty much patched things up, but Sharon was twenty years old, and she felt that it was time to get out on her own. She had a job at one of the stores on the Strand, and she was making enough money to pay for her own place, so Evelyn had told her to go for it.

It wasn't much of a place. The house was old, but it wasn't charming. In fact, it was pretty dilapidated. The steps sagged, and the Gulf Coast crud had eaten away at the paint and shingles. The yard was ragged, and the sidewalk was cracked and uneven. Christmas lights were strung along the gutter over the porch, and they blinked feebly in the twilight.

"I tried to get her to let me set her up in a better place," Dino said when we got out of my truck. "She wouldn't take the money."

The sky was darkening, and thick clouds were coming in from the Gulf. A damp breeze made it seem almost cold, and I could hear the shushing of the surf in the wind.

"She wants to make it on her own," I said. "You should understand that."

"I do. It's just that I want to help her."

She didn't want his help, and he should have understood that, too, but I didn't want to bring it up. We were there to talk about a party, not to improve his family relationships. I wasn't Dr. Laura.

"There's a light on up there," I said, "so she's probably at home."

"Yeah."

"You go first," I said, and he went to the side of the house, where there was a staircase leading up. He put a foot on the first step as if to test it.

"Haven't you been here before?" I asked.

"Just once. Evelyn brought me over right after Sharon moved in. I don't trust these steps."

"They'll hold you. Come on."

I went past him and up the steps. They seemed solid enough to me, though they creaked a little. I could hear Dino behind me, so I didn't look back.

At the top of the stairs there was a small landing, not much more than three feet square. I stood on it and knocked on the screen door.

A light came on, and I looked into the kitchen through the glass door top. Sharon was coming toward me across a worn and cracked yellow linoleum floor that had probably been laid down fifty years previously.

She looked better than the last time I'd seen her, but the circumstances had been quite different. None of us had looked too good then.

She snapped on an outside light, looked out at me. She was obviously surprised, and when she saw Dino standing on the step just below the landing, her eyes widened even more. She threw a dead bolt on the door, unlatched the screen, and pushed it open. I should have said something about the security value of a dead bolt on a door that was half glass, but I didn't want to upset Dino.

"What are you two doing here?" Sharon asked, as if she didn't know. She knew, though. I was sure of that.

"Tru wants to talk to you," Dino said. "Can we come in?"

She stepped aside to make room for us to come through the door.

"Sure," she said. "Come on in. Welcome to my happy home."

We went into the kitchen. The countertops were in worse shape than the linoleum. The porcelain on the side of the sink was cracked, and a big rusty spot was developing. The tiny refrigerator and stove were practically antiques, and I could see a couple of roach traps along the baseboard. The table was small and square, with a red Formica top. Around it were four chairs with curved steel frames and red vinyl seats and backs.

"Have a seat," Sharon said. "We can talk in here."

"I hope we're not interrupting anything," I said, taking one of the chairs.

She shrugged and sat opposite me. "I was just watching *The Simpsons*, but it was a rerun."

Dino sat beside her. "Tru wants to talk to you about that party. The one I called about last night."

Sharon looked at me. "He said you'd want to know about it. I guess I should have talked to the cops before now."

"No you shouldn't," Dino said.

" 'We don't go to the police,' " I said to Sharon. "Ever hear that one before?"

Sharon almost smiled. But not quite.

'I've heard it more than once," she said. "Look, Mr. Smith, I—"

"Wait," I said. "Let's just make it Tru, all right?"

"I . . . guess so. It's just that I'm a little uncomfortable talking to you."

I didn't blame her. If our positions had been reversed, I'd have been uncomfortable, too. Our last meeting hadn't been exactly under the best of conditions.

"Don't worry about it," I said. "Anything that happened was a long time ago. We've all changed since then. I've forgotten all about it."

I'd never forget it, but she didn't have to know that. Dino knew, though. I could tell by the way he was looking at me, but he was smart enough not to say anything.

"I wish none of that had ever happened," Sharon said. "I'm not proud of it."

"It's over and done with. I'm not interested in the past. Well, not that particular past. I'm more interested in what happened during spring break."

"I don't mind telling you about that, but I didn't do anything. I didn't really know that girl who died."

"Kelly Davis," I said. "That was her name."

"Like I said, I didn't really know her. She was with some guy, a football player. I didn't know him, either."

"Randall Kirbo," I said.

She thought about it. "I guess that was his name. There were lots of guys there."

I showed her Randall Kirbo's picture. "Him?"

"Yes, for sure."

"His name's Randall Kirbo. What about one named Chad Peavy?"

"I remember that name, too. I'm not sure which one he was."

"Another football player. He remembers you. There were a couple of others that you might have met. Patrick Mullen and Travis Bittner."

"I don't think so."

"It's not important right now. What I want you to tell me is what happened at that party."

"I don't remember much about it." She looked at Dino. "Why don't you go in the other room and see what's on TV?"

Dino wasn't much of a father, but he could take a hint. He stood up and said, "Do you have cable in this place?"

"That's about the only luxury I allow myself," Sharon said. "You can watch just about anything you're interested in. I get three different shopping channels."

"I hope that damn Juiceman isn't on," Dino said as he headed for the living room.

I found it hard to believe that someone who watched that manic exercise-machine pitchman could object to someone who sold juice, but maybe Dino just didn't like juice.

When he was gone and I could hear the TV from the other room, I said, "Now that he's gone, tell me why your memory seems a little impaired."

She looked over her shoulder as if to assure herself that Dino wasn't listening from the other room. When she turned back to me, there was a concerned look on her face.

"I want to help you," she said. "I guess maybe I feel like I owe it to you. But there's something you have to promise me."

I thought I knew what she wanted to hear. "Private detectives are like priests. Whatever you say to me is absolutely confidential. I won't even tell Dino."

"He might try to make you."

"You don't know Dino very well if you believe that."

"I *don't* know him very well. That's the point. And I don't want him going all fatherly on me."

"I'll keep him in line," I said, with more confidence than I felt. Obviously I wasn't the one who could predict what Dino might do.

But Sharon seemed to believe me. She said, "He was worried about me and about the drinking and drugs at that party. I might have exaggerated a little bit when I told him about it."

"How?" I asked.

"I didn't do any drugs. I told the truth about that, but I drank more than I told him. I wasn't drunk or anything, but I'd had more than just a glass of wine. So I don't really remember everything too well. I was worried about a term paper, and I guess I thought a few drinks would loosen me up."

"Did they?"

She laughed, but there wasn't much humor in it. I wondered how the term paper had turned out.

"I got pretty loose, all right," she said. "So loose, I wasn't even sure where I was for a while."

"But you saw Kelly Davis and Randall Kirbo together."

"I know I saw her. I know I even spent some time talking to her and some boy. It's what happened after that that I'm not sure of."

"What do you think happened?"

"There were some things going on upstairs," she said.

"What things?"

"That's where the drugs were."

Her eyes shifted, and I thought there might be more to it than that, but I couldn't figure out what.

"What kinds of drugs? Anything dangerous?"

"Ecstasy, I think. That can be weird. And pot, but that's all. Nothing really dangerous."

I was disappointed. I was hoping that the death of Kelly Davis could be tied into some kind of illegal substance. That would explain why Big Al was so eager to keep things quiet, and why Henry J. was paying visits to everyone involved.

Except Sharon. Something wasn't quite right here.

"You know Henry J.?" I asked.

She looked wary. "I've heard of him."

"Was he there that night?"

"Why should he have been?"

"Because he works for Big Al Pugh, and the party was at one of her beach houses."

"I wouldn't know about that," Sharon said. "Nobody said whose house it was."

I wasn't sure I believed that.

"So you didn't see Henry J.?"

"I don't think so."

"And he hasn't been around to see you since the party?"

"No. Why should he want to see me?"

"Because he might not like the idea of you talking about what went on there that night. Are you sure you didn't see him? He's older than any of the kids who were there, and probably bigger. His nose has been broken a lot."

More now than then, I thought.

"I might have seen somebody like that. I'm not sure. I was pretty wrecked, like I said."

"What about those drugs you mentioned? Who provided them? Could it have been Henry J.?"

"I don't think so. The drugs were just there, the way they are, you know?"

I didn't know, not really. Drug use hadn't been quite that casual when I was Sharon's age.

"How often do you go to parties like that one?" I asked.

"Not often. And I don't drink that much, either. It was just a one-time thing." She smiled. "You sound more like my father than Dino does."

"I don't mean to. I worry about people sometimes."

"Thanks, but you don't have to worry about me. I'm doing all right."

For some reason I believed her, at least about that. She wasn't the same young woman she'd been when we'd first met, and the change was for the better. I thought maybe she'd come to terms with who she really was, which is something a lot of us never quite manage.

Unfortunately, however, she wasn't turning out to be exactly the mine of information I'd hoped for, and I was almost certain that she was holding out on me. I asked if she could remember anything else about the party, anything at all, but I didn't get anymore out of her. After a few more minutes of trying, I called Dino.

"See anything you wanted to order?" I asked when he came back to the kitchen.

"Not a thing. Was Sharon any help to you?"

"Not much," Sharon said. "I couldn't remember a whole lot."

"So where does that leave us?" Dino asked me.

"It leaves us needing to see someone else."

"Who?"

"It's a surprise," I told him.

"Oh, boy," he said.

20

"I THOUGHT WE'D be going to see Evelyn," Dino said after we'd negotiated the run-down stairway and settled ourselves in the pickup.

"We are," I said. "I just didn't want to mention that in front of Sharon."

"Oh.

"I didn't want Sharon to think we didn't trust her," I said, starting the pickup and pulling away from the curb.

"But we do, don't we?"

"Mostly. But it never hurts to check."

"If you say so."

"I say so."

He didn't respond to that, and I drove over to the residential area near the Bolivar ferry landing. The streets in Evelyn's subdivision were all named for fish. I didn't know whether I'd rather live on a street named for a Romantic poet or a fish, but I was pretty sure that "Tuna" didn't have the same prestige as "Coleridge." Maybe it all depended on your priorities.

"How long's it been since you talked to Evelyn?" I asked when I stopped in front of her house.

"Not long. Couple of days."

"She'll be glad to see us, then," I said, and she was. She was also as surprised as Sharon.

"I don't know how you got him out of the house after dark, Tru," she said.

"It wasn't easy. I had to threaten to kill him."

Evelyn laughed at that, sure that I was kidding. She had a nice laugh.

"I'm afraid it's business instead of pleasure, though," I told her.

She wasn't one to waste time on small talk when there was business to be done. Maybe it was her background.

"Tell me about it," she said.

I told her the whole thing while Dino sat and looked at his hands. Now and then Evelyn would glance over at him and shake her head.

When I was finished, she said, "Old habits aren't easy to break. I hope you weren't too hard on him, Tru."

"Not as hard as I should have been."

"Good. But if anything like this ever happens again, he'd better go to the police or we'll both get after him. Now, what do you want from me?"

"I want to know if Sharon told you anything about that party."

"I wish she had, but she didn't. I suppose that when death is involved, she feels more comfortable with her father. He forgot to mention it to me, too."

"Hey," Dino said, coming out of his trance. "It's like you said. Old habits, and that stuff."

"I'd hoped you were doing better," Evelyn said.

"I'm trying. It's tough sometimes."

"I wish I could help you, Tru," Evelyn said. "But I don't know a thing."

"I was afraid of that. Well, Dino, are you ready to eat supper?"

"I guess so," he said.

He couldn't work up any real enthusiasm for the idea, however. I could tell that he'd rather go straight home.

"Can Evelyn go with us?" he asked.

"I don't think that would be a good idea. We'll still be working."

Dino grunted. "How can we work and eat?"

"We're going to the Hurricane Club," I said.

Dino nodded, as if he'd suspected as much. "Big Al's place."

"That's the one. I wonder if she'll be there."

"With my luck?" Dino said. "Sure she will."

WE WERE ONLY a short distance from the old downtown area, which had been going through something of a rebirth during the last few years. Of course, it would still be overrun by stragglers from the Dickens on the Strand celebrations, but the place we were going to was a little east of all the activity, in a part of town the tourists usually steered clear of, thanks to the fact that the lighting was bad and most of the buildings appeared in imminent danger of collapse. Not to mention that the people standing outside the buildings looked as if they were answering a casting call for the sequel to *Deliverance*.

The Hurricane Club had been in the same spot for almost as long as or maybe even longer than the Galvez Hotel had occupied its spot on the seawall. No one was really sure. It wasn't the kind of building whose owners were interested in requesting a historical marker from the state.

There were, of course, many differences in the Galvez and the Hurricane Club, the main one being that the Galvez received regular cleanings from a competent staff. I wasn't sure that the Hurricane Club had ever been cleaned at all.

I parked not far from the front entrance, and Dino and I got out of the truck. The establishment's name had once been painted on the wooden front of the building, but the paint was so faded that it was impossible to read in the darkness. The old wooden canopy over the door sagged dangerously, but the music coming from inside was pleasant. It was Patti Page singing "Cross over the Bridge." Big Al kept the jukebox stocked with things like that to keep out the riffraff. The local gang bangers couldn't stand it. Big Al considered them amateurs and had nothing to do with them.

Dino and I went inside, where it was almost as dark as it had been on the street, since most of the lighting came from four or five neon beer signs and the star on top of the little Christmas tree that stood on one end of the bar.

The tree was about the saddest I've ever seen. It made the one Charlie Brown picks out on his Christmas special look like the deluxe model. About half the needles had fallen out and they lay all around it on the bar. No one seemed to mind.

The dimness of the Hurricane Club's interior was probably just as well. There was no real way we could tell just how unsanitary the conditions were except by the smell, which was a mixture of stale cooking odors, cigarette smoke, wet sawdust, beer, and urine. In some places the sawdust was picturesque; in the Hurricane Club it was foul.

There were tables scattered around the one big room, and a short bar that had most likely been there since around the turn of the century. There were even a couple of brass spittoons near the bar. The spittoons were actually fairly clean, mainly because everyone apparently spit into the sawdust on the floor. I wouldn't have walked barefoot from the door to the bar for a thousand bucks. And if someone had wanted to cast a pirate movie, the Hurricane Club would have been a good place to look for extras. There was even a guy wearing an eye patch.

I fingered my tie. I knew that I was very overdressed, but I didn't think it would be a good idea to go home and change. If I did that, I wouldn't want to come back.

A thin haze of smoke hung just below the ceiling. Nearly everyone I saw was smoking. I don't think the Hurricane Club had a nonsmoking section.

Big Al was sitting at a table in the corner. Tonight her T-shirt said I LOVE ANIMALS. THEY'RE DELICIOUS.

Henry J. was there, too. His back was to us, but Big Al said something to him when we walked in and he turned around. He was wearing the same T-shirt he'd had on that afternoon, and I could see the bloodstains on it. They might have attracted attention at some place a little more respectable, say a cheap dive in Tijuana, but they didn't look out of place in the Hurricane Club.

Henry J.'s nose was covered with tape and something that winked in the dim light, some kind of metal brace I suspected. Although he didn't look overjoyed to see me, he started to get up to come over and greet me. Or to do something to me. But Big Al spoke to him and he sat back down. The two of them bent their heads together and whispered for a minute. Henry J. looked around at me once. He wasn't smiling.

Then the conversation was over, and Big Al motioned to us to join them.

"Be thinking about what you'd like to eat," I told Dino. "Remember, it's my treat."

He looked around, taking in the floor, and then he sniffed audibly.

"Treat?" he said.

"Sure. I said I'd buy your supper."

"I thought you were kidding when you said we'd eat here."

"Kidding? Me? It's not like I never bought you a meal before."

"Yeah, but not in any place like this."

"Best enchiladas in town. Or so I've heard."

"I'll bet you've never eaten one. Have you?"

"There's a first time for everything," I said, and led the way over to Big Al's table.

21

I COULD TELL by the look on his face, what I could see of it, that Henry J. didn't like me at all, but he didn't say a word to either me or Dino. He just sat there, staring at me as if he'd like to rip my heart out and feed it to a cat.

There was a cat handy, too, a big white one that slipped in from the kitchen, but it didn't appear to be in the market for a heart. There was already a sizable gray mouse dangling from its mouth.

"I assume that the two of you will join us for dinner," Big Al said.

I looked away from the cat. There was a plate of enchiladas, rice, and beans in front of Big Al. A covered dish of tortillas sat to one side, near a dish of picante sauce and a plastic basket of tortilla chips.

Henry J. must not have been hungry. There was no food in front of him, though there was a half-full bottle of Dos Equis to go with the three empty bottles beside it. Big Al was drinking Carta Blanca.

Dino and I sat down. Les Paul and Mary Ford came on the jukebox with "Mockingbird Hill."

"We'll have the enchiladas," I said. "I've heard they're really good."

"It's true," Big Al said. "Beer?"

"Not for me. Do you have Big Red?"

Big Al laughed. "We don't serve kids' drinks," she said.

"Water'll be fine, then. What about you, Dino?"

"Carta Blanca's OK."

Big Al waved a hand, and a man wearing an apron came over. The apron must have been white at one time, but the time had been years before I was born. He took our order and went into the kitchen. I looked around for the white cat, but it had disappeared. I hoped it hadn't gone back to the kitchen to deliver the meat for my enchiladas.

"You know," Big Al said to me, "you haven't been exactly nice to Henry J. lately."

"Henry J.'s been following me around," I said. "I don't like to be followed."

Big Al brought a forkful of enchilada to her mouth and stuffed it in. She chewed happily for a while, then took a hit from the Carta Blanca bottle.

She swallowed the beer and said, "That's the great thing about a free country. A man can go where he wants to go. On the other hand, a man can't assault someone for no reason at all. Look at poor Henry J.'s nose."

I looked, and in spite of the hate in Henry J.'s eyes, it wasn't easy not to laugh at his appearance.

"I have a feeling that whoever assaulted Henry J. did it for reasons of self-defense," I said.

Big Al waved her fork in the air. "Maybe. Maybe not. Why do I get the feeling you didn't come here to apologize?"

"Because I came here for the enchiladas?"

"Many people do," Big Al said.

I looked around the room. As far as I could tell, not a single person except Big Al was eating. Everyone else was drinking beer and listening to the jukebox, which was now playing "Rags to Riches," the Tony Bennett version.

"But not you," Big Al said.

The door to the kitchen opened. Our waiter came out, followed by the white cat, which was no longer carrying the mouse. I wish I hadn't seen him, to tell the truth.

"No," I said as the waiter set the thick white plates in front of us. "I didn't really come here to eat, but the food does look good."

The waiter used a folded towel to handle the plates, which were very hot. The enchiladas were covered with chopped onions and jalapeño peppers. The beans around the enchiladas bubbled and sizzled.

"If you didn't come for the food," Big Al said, "why did you come? Do you have a secret crush on me?"

"I'm sure there are a lot of guys who do," I said. "But I came to talk to you about a party."

"I thought we decided yesterday that we wouldn't discuss the party."

"We didn't decide anything," I said. "We just got interrupted."

I reached out for the picante sauce and spooned it onto the enchiladas. Dino watched me with a kind of horrified fascination, and I pushed the bowl over to him when I'd finished.

"I don't want any hot sauce," he said.

"Suit yourself."

I cut into the enchiladas and steam rose above the plate. I thought it might be best to wait a while before taking a bite, that is, unless I wanted to incinerate the inside of my mouth.

"About that party," I said.

"Big Al said we weren't going to talk about that," Henry J. said. He sounded particularly nasal, like a bad country and western singer.

"I'm talking to Big Al, not you," I told him.

He pushed his chair back about six inches, and I thought for a second that he was going to come across the table for me. But Big Al put up a hand, and he sat back down. I could tell he wasn't happy about it, though.

"Assuming that I have some idea of which party you're talking about," Big Al said, "why don't you tell me why you're so interested in it?"

"You know why," I said. "A girl was killed there."

"That's enough of that shit," Henry J. said, pushing his chair back at least a foot.

"Calm down, Henry J.," Big Al said. "This is getting interesting. I suppose you think you can prove what you're saying, Smith."

I couldn't prove anything, of course. I wasn't even sure I was right. I was just guessing to try to keep her off balance and maybe get her to say something in an unguarded moment, not that I thought she ever had any. I knew damned well that *something* had happened at that beach house, however, and that everyone was lying to me about it. I just didn't know what or why.

"Her name was Kelly Davis," I said. "You might have read about her in the newspaper."

Big Al shrugged her powerful shoulders and smiled.

"I might have," she said. "It seems to me that she was found in the Gulf. She drowned, I believe."

"No," I said. "She didn't drown."

"How did she die, then?"

I started to say that I didn't know, that the cause of death hadn't been discovered, but I didn't want to give her the satisfaction.

So I said, "She was murdered."

Big Al put her fork down on her plate with an audible clink.

"You don't know that."

"I believe it, and I'm going to prove it. And I'm going to find out what happened to Randall Kirbo, too."

"I never heard of him," Big Al said. "And now I'm tired of talking to you. Show them out, Henry J."

I would have gone quietly, and Dino would have, too. But Henry J. must not have thought so. Instead of politely standing up and asking us to leave, he shoved the table at me and hit me in the stomach so hard that my chair toppled over backward.

I landed hard and tried to bounce up so that I wouldn't have to lie too long in the sawdust that was clinging to me like a fungus. I was afraid it might eat right through my jacket.

I couldn't bounce anywhere, however, because I was tangled up with the chair. I tossed it aside just as Henry J. swung his Dos Equis bottle at Dino's head.

Dino put up his left forearm and knocked the bottle aside while throwing a short, hard right into Henry J.'s stomach. He should have known from his prior experience that hitting Henry J. in that particular spot would have about as much effect as hitting the bar. Some people are slow learners, however.

Henry J. grinned beneath his bandaged nose as if he hadn't even been touched and kicked Dino in the shin. Dino bent over, and Henry J. smashed a fist into the back of his neck. Dino crumpled, and Henry J. raised his foot to stomp him.

I was on my feet by then, and I grabbed my enchilada platter and threw it in Henry J.'s face. The food was still hot, and the plate was heavy. The combination didn't do Henry J.'s nose any good, but it didn't stop him, maybe because of the metal nose guard he was wearing. About all it did was mess up his bandage. He wiped a hand across his face and came at me.

I jumped aside, and Big Al hit me with a solid right just under the heart. It was a little like being kicked by a horse, and I staggered backward, my feet slipping in the sawdust.

Henry J. started to move in for the kill, but Dino stood up and got between us. Henry J. tried to kick him again. Dino did a little pirouette, grabbed his foot, and flipped him. I heard the crack when Henry J.'s head hit the floor. The sawdust apparently wasn't thick enough to serve as much of a buffer, but I didn't feel a bit sorry for Henry J. I didn't have time. Big Al was all over Dino, hitting him with a flurry of rights and lefts that was almost too fast to follow. He put up his arms and managed to stop most of the blows from landing solidly, but he was taking some damage.

I stepped over beside them and reached for Big Al's hair. It was awfully short, but I got a grip that allowed me to yank her backward.

She sounded like a snake with asthma as her breath hissed between her teeth, and she tried to twist around to hit me. She almost made it, but Dino grabbed her arm and twisted her back to face him. He was going to hit her, but he hesitated for just a fraction of a second, giving her time to drive her fist into his mouth.

He fell like a rock, and Big Al turned her attention to me again. She gave a powerful jerk of her head, and I was left with a tuft of her hair in my hand. I dropped it just as she hit me in the stomach.

I try to keep in shape. I run as often as I can, but running doesn't do much to harden the stomach. I bent double and gasped for breath.

Big Al didn't give me a chance to get one. She came on with a roundhouse punch that would most likely have killed me if I hadn't turned my head at the last second.

As it was, her knuckles scraped along my jawline, turning me almost around. I was still breathing as raggedly as a bronchitis victim on a coughing jag.

Big Al wound up again, but she wasn't going to have to hit me. There was someone else to do that for her. The bartender was right beside her, and he was holding a regulation Little League baseball bat. He fell into a crouch that made him look a little like Jeff Bagwell and took a swing at my head.

I dropped to my knees and the bat whistled through my hair. I really didn't like the idea of lying in the sawdust again, but I liked the idea of having my brains smeared on the bartender's bat even less. I rolled under a table and looked around.

Henry J. was sitting up, staring vaguely around. His head had struck the floor hard, and he didn't seem to have any idea where he was.

Dino was wrestling with Big Al. They were scuffling around in the sawdust.

The white cat was sitting by the kitchen door, watching calmly, as if he saw this kind of thing all the time. Most of the other patrons had disappeared. I wished I could.

The bartender was still after me. He yanked the table away and tossed it aside, then swung at me again, but I had my breath back, and I was able to stick a chair in his way. The bat splintered the chair back, and sent a stinging vibration all the way up the bartender's arms. He yelled and dropped the bat, wringing his hands.

The bat bounced off the sawdust. I grabbed it, stood up, and slammed it gently into the bartender's stomach, which was much softer than Henry J.'s. His eyes bugged, his tongue stuck out, and he gagged and sat down. Maybe I hadn't been as gentle as I'd thought.

Big Al had Dino down on the floor, pummeling his face. I gave her a shot in the kidney, and she rolled off him.

"Don't bother to get up," I said. "Dino and I will be leaving now. If we can. How about it, Dino?"

"Give me a couple of seconds," he said, sitting up. His face was already swelling a little.

Big Al measured me with her eyes, judging the chances of making a try for me. To my right, Henry J. was beginning to regain his senses. I slapped the bat lightly into the palm of my left hand, but I don't think I scared her a bit.

"I don't think you have a couple of seconds," I told Dino. "I think we should go right now."

He stood up, and I put my left hand under his arm, keeping a tight grip on the bat with my right. We backed toward the door like that, while Frankie Laine sang to us about the travails of being a moonlight gambler. The jukebox seemed very loud all of a sudden, but that was probably just my imagination, plus the fact that aside from the jukebox the club was almost completely silent now.

Big Al and Henry J. watched us leave. I wish I could say that they bid us an affectionate farewell, but that would be a slight exaggeration. The good news was that they didn't come after us. I'm sure neither of them felt like it, however, and so they let us go quietly. I hoped that there was no one waiting outside to curry favor with Big Al by tackling us and carrying us back in, but the sidewalk was deserted. Big Al had her supporters, but none of them had been in the Hurricane Club that evening, for which I was grateful.

When Dino and I got to the truck, I opened the door and helped him get in, tossing the bat in after him. I stumbled around to the driver's side and got in. In five seconds we were on our way.

When we got to Broadway, where the lights were brighter, Dino looked at the bat.

"This is a Ralph Kiner autograph model," he said. "It must be at least forty years old. I wonder how much it's worth?"

I wasn't in the mood to discuss baseball memorabilia. I was worried about what the sawdust on my clothes was going to do to the upholstery in the truck.

"You can have the bat if you want it," I said. "I don't think Big Al will be coming after it."

"She might. You can't tell about her and Henry J." He looked out at the esplanade for a second or two. "You know, I think Henry J. must be a little crazy."

"Really? What was your first clue?"

Dino took me seriously. "There was no call for him to do what he did in there. We weren't going to argue about leaving. Were we?"

"I wasn't."

"Me neither. I wonder if there's something he doesn't want Big Al to know?"

"It's a thought," I said.

He brushed at the legs of his jeans, knocking damp sawdust to the floor of the truck.

"I don't think this sawdust is very clean," he said.

"You're developing a real talent for stating the obvious."

"I'll bet people have been spitting in it for years. Decades, maybe. Can you smell it?"

I could smell it all right. The smell filled the whole truck. I just didn't want to think about it.

"You can take a bath when you get home," I said.

Dino put a hand to his face. His lips were swollen, and there was a bruise beginning to form on his jaw.

"I hope I don't get some incurable disease," he said.

"I'd recommend very hot water and an antibacterial soap if you have some."

"I think I do."

"Good. Use it."

He didn't say anything else for a few minutes, not until we were nearly at his house. Then he said, "There's one thing I gotta know, Tru."

"Go ahead and ask," I said.

"Would you really have eaten those enchiladas?"

I tried a smile. "We'll never know, will we?"

22

I LET DINO out at his house and drove home after he assured me that he was going to be just fine as soon he got a good night's sleep. I gave him the baseball bat and told him to take a couple of aspirin and call me in the morning, but he didn't laugh.

There were all kinds of ideas tumbling around in the back of my head by the time I got home, but I couldn't make sense of any of them. It was almost as if the bartender had hit me with that bat of his.

I managed to feed Nameless, take off my wetly sawdusted clothes and stick them in the washer, except for the jacket and tie, of course, which I hung on the back of a lawn chair outside. Maybe they'd air out and I could get them cleaned later.

After that, I took a hot shower, but I didn't manage to read even a page of O'Hara. I fell into the bed and went to sleep almost at once.

Nameless woke me up the next morning. He was standing on my stomach, plainly irritated that I hadn't gotten up at the usual time to feed him.

He stared at me accusingly with his green eyes and said, "Mowr."

I lifted my head to get a better look at him and immediately wished I hadn't. It felt as if it weighed a ton.

"Mowr," Nameless said again, with no regard for my pain. Cats have no pity.

"I don't guess I blame you for not feeling sorry for me," I told him. "I'd be upset if someone delayed my meals, too. But I've got a good excuse."

"Mowr?"

"Never mind. You wouldn't believe it, even if I told you."

"Mowr."

"Oh, sure, you say that now. But you haven't heard the story yet."

I tossed off the sheet and sat up with my legs over the side of the bed. My head felt a little better, but my whole body ached.

Nameless didn't care how I felt. He just wanted me to feed him. He jumped down from the bed and walked around in front of me so that he could look up at me.

"Mowr?"

"I'm not going to tell you. Let's just say that I'm getting too old to get into fights with women. And with bartenders who carry baseball bats."

Nameless had no comment. Apparently my decrepit condition was obvious to him. He stalked away, his tail in the air, confident that I would follow him.

So I took a deep breath, stood up, and did.

After I'd fed him, I shaved, then washed my clothes. I wasn't sure I'd ever wear them again, but I wanted them to be clean even if I threw them away. I didn't want to be arrested for polluting the garbage dump.

While the clothes were chugging through the Wash cycle, I went in and fixed a bowl of shredded wheat. It tasted surprisingly good, and I remembered that I hadn't eaten a thing since breakfast the previous day. I'd gotten cheated out of my enchiladas, but then, I hadn't paid for them, so I guess it all evened out. I finished the shredded wheat and had another bowl.

When I was finished, I put the bowl in the sink and ran water in it. Nameless hopped up on the drain board. I put a little soap in the bowl and washed it out with hot water. Then I dried it and put it away. Nameless gave me the accusing look that he'd been practicing.

"I've told you before," I said. "Drinking out of my bowls isn't sanitary."

He ignored me and got in the sink anyway. Since there was no bowl to drink from, he just licked the water in the bottom of the sink. You can't win with cats, so I left him there and went to run my clothes through another Wash cycle.

I put on my running shoes. I didn't feel like going for a run, but I went anyway. I wasn't going to let a little thing like a few hundred bruises stop me. I was old and decrepit, but I wasn't going to give up my exercise. Not yet, anyway.

When I got outside, I discovered that the weather had undergone a complete change. Gray clouds scudded along so close to my head that I could have jumped up and touched them, if I could have jumped, which wasn't very likely. The air was heavy with moisture, and a cold wind blew from the north. I didn't mind. It was pretty good weather for a run.

I ran about three miles with only an occasional twinge from my bad knee, and by the time I got back to the house I was feeling much better. The run had loosened me up and relaxed my muscles. A hot shower relaxed me even further, and after I dried off I sat down to think things over.

I'd put in a hard day on Sunday, but I wasn't sure I had much to show for it. About the only conclusion I'd come to was that nearly everyone was still lying to me. Maybe not Dino, but I thought his daughter was. And I was absolutely certain that Patrick Mullen and Chad Peavy were. Everyone was covering up something, and I wondered if all of them had played some role or another in the death of Kelly Davis. I hoped not, especially in Sharon's case, but I didn't know what else to think. It was depressing.

Even more depressing was the fact that I knew no more about what had happened to Randall Kirbo than I'd known when I started out.

What I did know was that Big Al was involved in both cases. Or maybe I didn't even know that. Maybe only Henry J. was involved. Dino's idea about Henry J.'s overreaction made sense when I thought about it. Dino had overreacted in the same way when he'd wanted to put an end to a conversation. That could explain some of Henry J.'s behavior, I thought, but not all of it.

I was also sure that in all the lying, someone had told me the truth about something important, something that should have meant something to me, but for the life of me I couldn't figure out what it was.

I didn't know what to do next, so I looked through the notes I'd made in the police station. I'd taken down the address and phone number of Kelly Davis's parents. I didn't feel like making the long drive to San Antonio to interview them in person, but I could call.

The mother answered the phone. Kelly's father was at work, she said, but after I explained who I was and what I was working on, and told her that I'd spoken to Bob Lattner about things, she said that she'd be glad to talk to me if I thought I could do anything about Kelly's death.

"Someone killed her," she said. "And I want that person punished. I want that person to suffer a little of the hell I've gone through for the last nine months."

"I don't know that I can do anything about that," I said. "I've really been hired only to find out what happened to Randall Kirbo."

"I can understand why his parents are concerned," she said. "Bob thinks he's dead, too."

I assumed that would be Uncle Bob, the cop.

"Did he say why?" I asked.

"He says that whoever killed Kelly probably killed the Kirbo boy, too. He says they put them both in the Gulf, and that Kelly just happened to be the one who was found."

Old Uncle Bob hadn't shared that thought with me. I wondered why, aside from the fact that he didn't seem to like me very much at all, a fact I had neglected to mention to Mrs. Davis.

"Bob really loved Kelly," she went on. "She was his favorite niece. He loves Kate and Karen, too, of course, but Kelly was always the one he doted on."

Good old Bob hadn't mentioned that, either. I'd been worried from the beginning about the possibility of his emotional involvement in the case, and Mrs. Davis had done absolutely nothing to relieve my misgivings.

"Kate and Karen were Kelly's sisters?" I said.

"Yes. They're still in high school, and I'll never let them go on spring break when they get to college. You can count on that."

I didn't blame her. I said, "Did Kelly call you while she was here in Galveston?"

"Yes. She called twice to tell us that she was all right and to tell us what a good time she was having."

Mrs. Davis had to pause for a second while she tried to stop remembering, something that's not always easy. Sometimes it's just downright impossible.

"I don't know what happened that night," she went on after a while. "All I know is what Bob told us. She went to a party, and she met some boys there. He talked to some of them, but they didn't tell him anything. Or so he said."

"Why do you put it that way?" I asked.

I could hear her breathing while she thought about it.

"He just seemed vague when I talked to him," she said finally. "It was as if he really did know something, but he didn't want to tell me."

I filed that away under "Other Stuff I'd Like to Discuss with Uncle Bob."

"Did he tell you any of the boys' names?" I asked. "Had Kelly known any of them before?"

"One of them was named Chad," she said. "I don't remember his last name, and I don't think Kelly knew him."

"That's OK. I've met him."

"What kind of boy is he?"

"I'm not sure," I said.

"Sometimes I think I'd like to talk to them, just to ask them what she was like that night. You know. Was she having a good time? Was she behaving herself? She was a good girl, Mr. Smith. She really was. She would never have done anything to cause someone to kill her."

There was nothing I could say to that, nothing comforting, at any rate. The truth was that you could never be sure what someone might do, even someone you thought you knew very well indeed. I'd had some experience along those lines. More than I'd ever wanted to have, as a matter of fact.

"You can see the problem, can't you?" Mrs. Davis said.

I could see it all right. A bunch of all-American kids at an all-American party, just having a good time without any intent to harm anyone at all. But it hadn't been that way. It couldn't have been that way. If it had, Kelly Davis would still be alive, and I wouldn't be having this conversation.

"Did Kelly drink?" I asked.

"She did at that party," Mrs. Davis said. "There was alcohol in her blood. But not much, not even enough to make her legally drunk, much less to impair her judgment. That's why I have so much trouble with the whole thing, Mr. Smith. It just doesn't make sense."

We talked a while longer, and after I hung up the phone I thought over every conversation I'd had since meeting the Kirbos. As far as I could tell, everyone involved in the whole mess was a wonderful person, highly moral, a good student, and a model son or daughter who would never even have thought of doing anything wrong.

With the notable exceptions, of course, of Big Al and Henry J. No one would mistake them for prototypes of rectitude.

Which didn't mean they'd killed Kelly Davis. They seemed to be lacking one essential requirement.

They didn't have a motive.

I had to agree with Mrs. Davis about one thing for sure. It just didn't make sense.

23

WHEN YOU DON'T know where else to turn, go to the cops, that's my motto. It really isn't, of course, but I like thinking of it that way since the very idea drives Dino crazy.

I called Gerald Barnes, who said he'd be glad to talk to me. Well, maybe "glad" wasn't exactly the word he used, but he did say that he didn't mind if I came by, as long as I had something to tell him that might be important. After all, he was a very busy man.

He didn't look especially busy when I saw him sitting at his desk. He just seemed to be pushing some papers around, but I didn't think I'd try staying any longer than a few minutes. I didn't want to impose on his good nature any more than necessary.

"So what's new, Smith?" he asked when he looked up and saw me.

"Nothing," I said. "That's the problem."

"Things not going quite the way you thought?"

I sat in the chair by his desk. "Nope. I thought maybe you could help me out a little."

He looked genuinely puzzled. "How could I do that?"

"I want to know about Bob Lattner," I said.

As usual, Barnes looked around to see who was listening. Maybe he was paranoid. Or maybe all cops are. At any rate, no one seemed to have the least interest in us. Everyone had a report to fill out or someone to question, or a coffee cup to fill.

"What do you want to know?" he asked.

"I want to know how he happened to get assigned to a case that he was personally involved in. I didn't think that was allowed, as a general rule."

"I don't know about any rules like that. Not any written rules, anyway. Besides, when he got assigned to the Kirbo disappearance, there was no involvement. Officially, there's still not."

"Did he put in a lot of hours?"

"I wouldn't know about that."

"Yes, you would."

He didn't take the bait. He said, "Why do you want to know?"

"It's just an idea that I'm working on."

"But you're not going to share it with me, are you?"

I smiled ingratiatingly. "Maybe later."

"Sure. I know what that means. It means never."

"I've helped you out before, haven't I?"

"Some," he admitted.

"Then you can help me out a little this time."

"All right. He worked darn hard on the Kirbo thing. He put in a lot of hours for a while. What are you on to, Smith?"

"Probably nothing," I said, and it was the truth. "Nothing seems right about the whole thing, and I'm only trying to make some sense of it."

It was an evasive answer, and he saw right through it. He let it slide, however.

"Something's worrying you, though. Am I right?"

"You're right. I can't even figure out how Big Al and Henry J. figure in."

"Maybe they don't. Big Al is involved in plenty of things, all of them bad, but that doesn't mean she had anything to do with this."

"The party was at one of her houses."

"She rents out houses all the time. Half the restaurants in town have her ads stuck up on bulletin boards."

"Henry J.'s been following me."

"So? If you've been sticking your nose in Big Al's business, Henry J.'s going to try to stop you. You should know that." He smiled and pushed up his glasses. "And speaking of noses, I understand that Henry J. has some new nose problems. And that someone started a fight with him and Big Al last night at the Hurricane Club."

"You've been talking to your CIs," I said.

"More crimes have been solved by using confidential informants than by computers, fingerprint experts, forensic pathologists—you name it. Don't knock CIs."

"I wasn't knocking them. I was paying you a compliment."

"I know. And I think you're on the right track with Big Al. She likes to keep a low profile, and getting into a brawl at her own club isn't a good way to do that. Half the people who were in there last night have called here today to tell someone about it."

"I don't think it was her idea. You wouldn't know whether Henry J.'s been branching out on his own, would you?"

Barnes looked at the ceiling, then down at the top of his desk.

"That's an interesting question," he said.

There was nothing very interesting there that I could see, but then he said, "What made you ask it?"

"I was just curious."

"There you go again, being a wiseass at the wrong time. You should try telling the truth from time to time, Smith. You might find out more that way."

I didn't think so, but I didn't want to get into a philosophical argument with him.

"I'm sorry. It's just a bad habit I've picked up from Dino."

He gave me a look and said, "I'll let that one pass. But you might be on to something. I don't know what, though."

"Then why do you think I'm on to something?"

"Just rumors. And pretty vague ones at that. Do you know what the relationship between Big Al and Henry J. is?"

"I don't think anyone knows that for sure. He's obviously some kind of bodyguard, but I don't know if there's more to it than that."

Barnes looked around the room again. There was still no more interest in me than if I were a piece of furniture.

"Let's go outside," Barnes said. "I don't really like to talk in here."

The weather hadn't improved a bit. If anything, it was getting worse. There was a light mist that clung to my face and my sweatshirt and settled in my hair.

"We can sit in your truck," Barnes said.

I was glad that, for the most part, the tourists had cleared off the Island and there had been plenty of parking spaces on the street. It would have been embarrassing if I'd been parked in someone's private spot.

When we were both in the truck and had closed the doors, I lowered my window about an inch so that the windows wouldn't fog up while we talked.

"What's the big secret?" I asked.

"Nothing, really," Barnes said. "But Big Al has ears everywhere, and I don't want her hearing about this."

"About what?"

"About the fact that I've found out some things that even she might not know."

"I thought she had ears everywhere."

"She does, but I might be one step ahead of her this time. You probably know that she's into a little bit of everything crooked on the Island."

"No!" I said. "You're kidding. I'm shocked."

"Knock it off, will you?"

I knocked it off. I said, "Whatever she's doing now, she's been doing for twenty years, but no one's stopped her."

"I didn't say I was going to stop *her*. I don't remember saying that I was going to stop anyone."

"All right. I'm getting ahead of you. Why don't you just tell me what the deal is."

He leaned against the passenger door. "The deal is that Henry J. is branching out. He's been doing a little business of his own, and he's not as smart as Big Al. He's been careless."

"What kind of business?" I asked.

"The drug business. Big Al controls plenty of that action herself, of course, but we think Henry J.'s been cutting himself in lately. He's always been the middleman, but now he's the end of the line."

"And Big Al doesn't know?"

"I don't think so. It's just nickel-and-dime stuff. Walking-around money."

"Which brings us back to your original question. What's the relationship between Big Al and Henry J.?"

"Nobody knows that for sure, but whatever it is, there's been a little breakdown in the last few months. And that's what I'm going to use to get them both. I hope."

"Where does that leave me?" I asked.

"It leaves you where you'd better not screw things up for me. That's where it leaves you."

I didn't want to screw things up, but I was already wondering what this little bit of information meant to me and how I could use it. It certainly seemed to back up the suspicions I was beginning to develop about Henry J.

"There's one person here in town who might be able to tell you a little more about those two," Barnes said.

"What two?"

"Who do you think? The two we've been talking about. Big Al and Henry J."

"Right. And who's this person who can tell me about them?"

Barnes smiled and said, "It's someone you know pretty well."

"Dino," I said, thinking that my old friend had suckered me again.

But Barnes fooled me. He said, "No, it's not Dino. It's a woman."

I was already tired of guessing, so I said, "Look, just go ahead and tell me."

"Sure," Barnes said. "It's Cathy Macklin."

24

MOISTURE HAD CONDENSED on the inside of the truck windows in spite of my having left an air space. Barnes was just a gray blur as he walked back across the shiny black parking lot to the police station.

I opened the glove compartment and found a little packet of tissues, got one out, and rubbed the windshield until I could see through it more clearly. I couldn't just sit there all day, so I started the truck and drove up to the seawall, where I turned right and headed west. Before I'd gone very far, the heater had cleared the windows completely, and I devoted my time to thinking about Cathy Macklin.

Cathy was Braddy Macklin's daughter, and Braddy had been a bodyguard for Dino's uncles back in the good old days, or the not-so-good old days, depending on your point of view. He'd been tough and mean and ruthless and perfect for the job, but he'd gotten old and slowed down some, and someone had killed him. It was because of his murder that I'd met Cathy.

It stood to reason that she would know Big Al. Her father had known just about everyone involved in the shady side of Galveston life, and some of them had been his good friends. Whether I wanted to talk to Cathy about one of those friends was the question I had to answer.

I drove west along Seawall Boulevard, which was practically deserted. No one wanted to go outside on such a gloomy day. The S-10's headlights seemed to be absorbed into the wet black street. The dark water of the Gulf slapped into the pilings of the Island Retreat and rolled up on the beach.

Cathy had inherited a motel from her father. It was about the only thing of value he'd left to her, but she did a good business most of the time, especially considering that the location wasn't one of the best on the Island. It was down on the west end, just past the area that had once been an army post, Fort Crockett. If you looked closely when you drove past, you could still identify some of the old army buildings, but most people had forgotten the post was ever there.

Cathy's motel, the Seawall Courts, was designed to look like a tourist court out of the 1940s. It was composed of individual stucco units on tall legs, and all the units stood in a low area behind the seawall. I supposed that the people who stayed there got a cheap thrill from the idea that in case of a flood they would be stranded in their rooms until the water went down, but it didn't hold much appeal for me.

I stopped the truck beside the stairs leading up to the manager's unit, where Cathy lived. I hadn't called her in weeks, and I didn't know what to say to her. I sat in the truck for a minute, trying to think of something, and while I was waiting, the clouds opened up. The mist turned to a downpour that drummed on the Chevy's metal roof, and I could hardly see past the end of the hood. Just what I needed, I thought. A flood.

I don't carry an umbrella in the truck. I never use one. It just isn't worth the trouble. Sure, an umbrella works pretty well when you're getting out of a vehicle if the wind doesn't turn it inside out within ten seconds, but when you're getting back in and trying to fold the umbrella down at the same time, you usually get as wet as you would have if you hadn't had any cover at all.

I got out of the truck and dashed up the stairs. The rain plastered my hair to my head and soaked through my sweatshirt before I reached the top, where there was a covered landing. I stood there feeling like someone had thrown a bucket of ice water on me and rang the bell.

Cathy came to the door. Her eyes widened when she saw me, either because she'd been expecting a customer or because I looked like someone who'd just swum across the Gulf from the east coast of Florida.

"You'd better come in," she said, opening the door.

I stepped inside the office, which didn't really look like an office at all. There was a desk with a computer on it, some potted plants that looked as if they might be slightly overwatered, a couple of overstuffed chairs, and a small table that held a coffee maker and some Styrofoam cups. That was about all. You don't need much when you run a small operation. I stood there, dripping on the rug.

"I'll be back in a second," Cathy said. She left the room and when she came back, she was carrying a large white towel. She handed the towel to me, and I started drying off.

Cathy watched me with a bemused look. She had dark hair with only a touch of gray in it and very blue eyes. I was a sucker for blue eyes. Among other things.

I dried my hair and face, but I couldn't do much about my clothes. I handed her the towel and said, "Thanks."

"You're welcome." She draped the towel over the back of the chair at the computer desk. "To what do I owe the honor of this unexpected visit?"

"I guess I should have called," I said.

"You haven't been doing a lot of that lately."

"I know. I . . ."

I stopped because I didn't have any idea what to say next. My social skills seemed to have deteriorated seriously.

"I talked to Dino not long ago," she said. "He told me that you'd had a little trouble with some old friends."

I hadn't known that Dino was discussing my personal life with Cathy. But then he probably didn't know that I was discussing his personal life with Evelyn, either.

"It had to do with prairie chickens," I said. "And some people I knew a long time ago."

"One of them was a woman."

I decided that I was definitely going to kill Dino. He was becoming a real aggravation to me.

"She was someone I knew in high school," I said. "She'd changed. Or maybe she hadn't."

Cathy laughed. "Haven't we all changed?" she said.

I wasn't sure, but I said, "I guess so. Have you had lunch?"

"Yes, and I just happen to have a little something left over. Would you like to eat?"

"Sure." One of my problems was that I didn't eat regularly. "That is, if you don't mind."

"I don't mind. It'll be nice to have someone to talk to on a day like this."

She led the way to her small kitchen, which held a wooden table big enough for only two chairs. I sat in one of them while she rummaged around in the refrigerator.

"Cold Virginia ham, a little cheese, a few carrot sticks, and some homemade whole wheat bread," she said, setting a plate on the table in front of me. "I don't have any Big Red, but I can offer you some wonderful tap water."

"Water is fine." I looked at the bread. "I didn't know you were a baker."

"I bought a bread machine. I've probably gained five pounds in the last two weeks."

If she'd gained any weight at all, I couldn't tell. Her jeans seemed to fit her with rigorous precision. When I began to eat, she sat in the chair opposite me, put her elbows on the table, and leaned forward.

"Now," she said, "tell me why you're here."

"I wanted to see you," I said.

"And I'm glad. But somehow I think there's more to it than that."

The ham was tender and tasty, and the cheese was mellow. The bread tasted like the loaves my grandmother used to bake in her oven when I was eight or nine years old. I hated to spoil the food and the good feeling I had about being with Cathy again by talking about the case, but I didn't really have any choice. So I just plunged right in.

"I'm working on something that involves Big Al Pugh and Henry J.," I said.

"I thought it must be something you were working on."

"It's not that I didn't want to call you or come by," I said. "It's . . . well, it's sort of hard to explain."

"Look, Tru, you've told me all about your sister and how you think you didn't come through for her. But that was a long time ago, and it's time you got over it. Besides, you had no way of knowing that she was in any danger. You can't save the world all by yourself."

I knew that. It was why I'd quit trying.

"And you can't just hide yourself in that old house of Dino's, either," Cathy went on as if she'd read my mind. "What good does it do you to bury yourself out there?"

I'd asked myself that question often enough, but I couldn't answer it. It was easy for me to see that Dino needed to get a life. It was a lot harder to realize that I needed one, too. And on those days when I realized it, it was almost impossible to make myself want to do anything about it.

"Well?" Cathy said.

I held up what was left of the slice of whole wheat bread she'd given me.

"This is great bread," I told her.

She leaned back in her chair, crossing her arms in front of her. A bad sign.

"I'm not going to let you off that easily," she said. "I'm not going to tell you what you want to know until you promise me you'll begin getting out more. Maybe coming into town once a day. You don't have to come by and see me. You don't have to see me at all. But you have to do *something*."

It would be an easy promise to make. But it wouldn't be easy to keep.

"How about if we try something simpler?" I asked. "I promise I'll come to see you at least once a week, maybe take you out to dinner or to a movie. That is, if you want to see me that often."

She uncrossed her arms. "Oh, I want to see you, Tru. I want to see you very much. I'm just not sure you want to see me."

"I do. I just have trouble with my follow-through now and then."

"How do I know you're not just saying that because you want me to tell you something about Big Al? Or because you like my whole wheat bread?"

"I like the bread, all right," I said. "I've eaten two slices."

"Don't joke about this, Tru."

"You're right. I shouldn't joke. I meant what I said, and I didn't say it just to get you to tell me something or just because I like your cooking. I said it because I like you and because I want to see you more often."

"Are you sure?"

"Trust me," I said.

She leaned forward on to the table again and her face relaxed into a smile.

"I guess I'll have to," she said.

25

BIG AL HAD met Henry J. in high school, and they had immediately known they were soul mates.

"They both liked to work out," Cathy said. "They both liked to pick on the kids who were smaller and weaker. They both liked to sneak through the teachers' parking lot and key their cars."

"Just your normal teenagers," I said.

"Not exactly. Did you know that Big Al started her career in high school?"

"No. But it makes sense. She's been on the shady side of the law for as long as anyone remembers."

"She sold dope on the school campus. They never caught her, though."

"How did she get away with it?"

We'd moved from the kitchen to the living room, and we were sitting on the couch, halfway watching the football game while Cathy told me what she knew about Big Al. I didn't pay much attention to football these days, but it appeared that the Dallas Cowboys were heading into the play-offs again if they could manage to keep the majority of their starters out of jail until after the season was over.

"Big Al got away with a lot of things because she was smart," Cathy said. "And she got away with a lot more because Henry J. wasn't."

"That doesn't exactly make sense," I said.

Cathy disagreed. "Of course it does. Think about it."

I thought about it, but I didn't get anywhere. Neither did the Cowboys, who had just run three notably unsuccessful plays, losing big yardage. They were forced to punt from their own ten. Maybe they weren't going to the play-offs after all.

"Are you thinking, or are you watching that game?" Cathy asked.

"Both," I said. "But I can't come up with an answer."

"Big Al let Henry J. take the falls for her. That's how. He spent a lot of time in court and never graduated from high school. But Big Al did."

"She must have stuck by him, though," I said. "They're still together."

"Wouldn't you stick by someone who wasn't smart enough to figure out how he was being used? You'd never know when you'd want to use him again."

"I don't remember hearing about Henry J. doing any jail time lately. Or ever, for that matter."

"He hasn't, as far as I know. But that doesn't mean he won't."

"Let me see if I've got this straight," I said. "Henry J. and Big Al are a team. Big Al is the brains, and Henry J. is the fall guy. But he's also the enforcer."

"You've heard about Henry J.'s escapades," Cathy said. "I think all the stories are true."

"So he's loyal but dumb. If someone needs killing, he does the job."

"That's about the size of it."

"So what happens when someone like Henry J. finally catches on?" I asked. "Maybe he's even thought all along that he was the one in control, that he was calling the shots. But he finds out that a woman is running the show and that she's playing him for a sucker."

"I don't know how the macho male mind works," Cathy said. "I guess you'll have to tell me. What happens?"

"You're implying that I *do* know how the macho male mind works?"

"Let's just say that you'd have a better idea than I would. How's that?"

"It'll have to do. OK, I'll tell you. If you're a guy like Henry J., you get angry, and you try to get a little of your own back. Maybe you dip in the till if you're smart enough to figure out how it's done, which Henry J. isn't. Or maybe you try to branch out on your own, just to prove you're your own man. That doesn't require brains. Just the opposite, in fact. If Big Al caught someone doing that, she'd give him a cheap sex-change operation."

Cathy didn't know whether Henry J. was operating on his own or not. She hadn't had any contact with Big Al since Braddy's death, and she didn't want any. She didn't see her father's past or the people connected with it as being romantic in the least, the way some people might.

We talked about Big Al for a bit longer, but I didn't learn anything more. Then our conversation drifted on to other, more personal areas, and one thing led to another. I didn't see the end of the football game, but then, it hadn't been very interesting anyway. It was getting late when I left, with a promise that I would call the next day.

"And you'd better not let me down," Cathy said as I walked down the stairs.

I stopped at the bottom, put my hand over my heart, and told her I was a changed man.

She laughed as she closed the door.

THE RAIN HAD stopped, but the sky still hung down within jumping distance. The clouds were so dark and heavy that it might as well have been night, though it was only a little after five o'clock.

I drove home feeling much better about things, at least as far as Cathy was concerned. I still didn't have a handle on what had happened to Randall Kirbo, but I was getting a lot of information. Maybe sooner or later some of it would form a pattern that I could recognize.

I fed Nameless, put some CDs on the changer, and sat down to try to make sense of things.

One theory went like this: Henry J. was getting tired of being pushed around by Big Al, who was even more macho than he was, so he tried his hand at selling a little dope to college kids, maybe to get enough money together to branch out on his own. Fine. But what did that have to do with Randall Kirbo and Kelly Davis? I didn't have a clue, which was the flaw in that theory.

Another theory was that Bob Lattner was involved somehow. Kelly Davis was his favorite niece. If Randall Kirbo had anything to do with her death, and if Lattner had found out about it, he might have decided that the law didn't move fast enough to suit him. So he'd killed Kirbo and dumped his body somewhere. There were lots of places better than the Gulf. That all made a lot of sense to me, considering what I'd seen of Lattner's personality, but it was assuming a lot of things I didn't know.

So much for my theories.

I still had the nagging feeling that there was some little fact that I'd missed, something I'd let slip by me as insignificant or even meaningless but that would turn out to be the key to everything.

I thought about it while I listened to the Diamonds singing "The Stroll." A wonderful song, but nothing they said was any help to me. I leaned back in the recliner, and I was just about to go to sleep when the telephone rang. I started to ignore it, but I didn't think that would be a good idea. You never know what might be important.

I answered, and it was Dino, who was practically incoherent. I got enough of what he was yelling at me to know that he thought someone was trying to kill Sharon and that he wanted me to get to her place quick.

He didn't have to tell me twice.

26

SEAWALL BOULEVARD IS long and straight and perfect for speeding if no one's out driving around and there aren't any patrol cars lurking on the side streets. I didn't see any patrol cars, and I was practically flying low when I turned off on the street that led to Sharon's apartment. I'm pretty sure that the tires on my side of the truck weren't touching the street at all during the turn.

It was dark and quiet at Sharon's. No police, of course. ("We don't go to the cops.") Dino's old Pontiac was already parked out front, but then he lives closer than I do, and it was his daughter someone was trying to kill.

Or maybe not. I didn't see any signs of imminent death as I stepped out of the truck. I walked down the block, but there was no flurry of agitation in the area.

The streetlight at the corner was burned out, but there was nothing particularly unusual about that. In any good-sized town streetlights burned out all the time.

None of the neighbors was standing out in the street, flashlight in hand, trying to figure out what was going on.

No dogs were barking furiously in the darkness as if an intruder were running through back alleys.

There were no fences full of arching cats with tails puffed out to the size of feather dusters.

All in all, it was a quiet evening. Cold and unpleasant, yes, but quiet and not threatening in any way that I could determine. But then I hadn't talked to Sharon yet.

I went up the stairs and knocked. Dino let me in.

"You'd think anyone would know better than to have a door with a big pane of glass in the top of it," he said. "What good does a dead bolt do in a door like this, anyway?"

I'd wondered the same thing the previous day, but I hadn't said anything. Anyone who wanted in would just have to knock out the glass, reach in, and turn the bolt.

In fact, it appeared that someone had done just that. There was broken glass all over the worn linoleum, and a few shards stuck dangerously out of the door frame.

"Where's Sharon?" I asked. "Is she OK?"

"She's in the other room, and she's OK," Dino said. "But I'm not sure I am."

"I guess I should have asked about you first."

"You never let up, do you, Tru?"

"Sorry," I said. "Sometimes I'm a little too flippant."

"Flippant? What the hell does that mean? Who uses words like that at a time like this?"

What Dino needed was a good jolt of something soothing, but Sharon probably didn't have any Big Red.

"Why don't you go sit in the living room and send Sharon in here," I said.

The idea didn't appeal to Dino in the least. He said, "I got enough of that last night. I want to hear what she has to say."

"I'll make a deal with you. You go in there, and we'll talk in here. If there's anything you need to hear, I'll call you."

"You can be a real asshole sometimes, Tru."

"So everyone loves to tell me."

"Well, they're all right about you."

"I think it's just a matter of opinion, but I won't argue with you about it. Now, send Sharon in here."

He went out, looking as if he'd like to deck me, which he probably would. There was no one else around for him to take his fear and frustration out on, except for Sharon, and Dino had never hit a woman in his life, unless of course you counted Big Al, which at the moment I didn't feel inclined to do.

Sharon came in. There were a few shallow cuts on her face, and one that had been covered with a plastic bandage.

"Someone shot at me," she said.

"Are you sure?"

It was a stupid question, and I deserved the look she gave me.

"OK," I said. "You're sure. Where were you?"

"I was standing by the door." She pointed toward the door I'd just walked through, where all the glass was on the floor. "Someone had made a noise downstairs, and I looked out to see what was going on."

"What kind of noise?"

"It sounded like he kicked over the garbage cans. They're right down there under the stairs."

"And when you looked through the glass, someone shot at you?"

"That's right. Glass went everywhere." She touched the bandage with a finger. "I'm lucky I wasn't cut worse."

"You're lucky you weren't killed," I told her.

I went over to the door and looked outside. The street slanted sharply downhill toward Broadway, and someone standing on the sidewalk halfway down the block would have had a fairly clear shot. Shooting uphill is a tricky proposition, however, for someone who hasn't had much practice at it.

"Did you hear the shot?" I asked.

She frowned. "I'm not sure. With the glass breaking and everything, I wasn't really listening."

"What happened after the glass broke?"

"I fell down. I was scared, and I thought I was hurt worse than I am. Then I called Dino."

Whoever had fired the shot hadn't hung around to see for sure if he'd done the job he'd set out to do, not that I blamed him. Someone might have reported the gunfire. On the other hand, it might not have been reported at all. What's one more noise on a cold winter's night?

I looked up at the ceiling. It was stained by smoke and grease from years of cooking on the tiny stove, but I thought I could see where the bullet had gone in. There was no need to get it out immediately. It would stay there for a while.

I didn't even bother to ask if she'd called the police, which would have been a really foolish question, but I did ask if she'd seen anyone or anything when she looked out the window.

"It was too dark. And the streetlight's out."

I'd noticed that. Maybe it hadn't burned out after all. A rock would have done the job if someone hadn't wanted to risk an extra shot.

"Is there anything you'd like to tell me about that spring break party?" I asked. "Anything that you might have remembered since last night?"

She shook her head, then looked over her shoulder. Turning back to me, she said, "There might be one thing."

I waited.

"There was more going on upstairs at that party than I said."

"More than drugs?"

"Sex."

"Excuse me if I'm not shocked," I said.

"You might be if you knew what kind of sex I'm talking about."

"There's more than one kind?"

"Dino always says you're a smart-ass."

"He meant that I'm flippant. That's the word he prefers. You could ask him."

"Whatever. Anyway, I'm talking about forced sex."

That put a new slant on things, all right, but I wasn't exactly sure what she was talking about.

"You'd better explain that," I said.

"So you don't know as much as you think you do," she said.

"I hardly ever do."

"I believe you. Anyway, I'm really talking about drugs again. Have you ever heard of Liquid X?"

I'd heard of it. It went by other names, too, Easy Lay and Grievous Bodily Harm were a couple of them. It was really gamma y-hydroxy butyrate, GHB. It was supposed to be a powerful Mickey Finn, and there were men who slipped it into women's drinks as an aid to date rape. The drug not only made them helpless to fight off an attack, it supposedly wiped out any memory of the experience.

"Who was using it?" I asked.

"I don't know for sure. When I found out about it, I got out of there. I wasn't feeling any too good by then, and when some girl told me that it was being slipped into some of the drinks, I knew it was time for me to leave."

She looked at me with perfect innocence, so perfect, in fact, that I was sure there was more to the story.

So I looked back at her and said, "Do you want to tell me the rest of it, or do you want me to call Dino in here?"

"You're worse than I thought," she said.

"I guarantee it. So tell me."

"They were getting the drug from Henry J.," she said.

27

"I'LL KILL THE son of a bitch," Dino said, raging out of the living room, where he'd no doubt been standing by the door and listening to every word.

I grabbed his arm as he brushed by me. "Didn't anyone ever tell you that it's not polite to eavesdrop?" I asked him.

He didn't even slow down. He shook off my hand and went out the door, letting it slam behind him.

"Stop him," Sharon said.

I told her that I'd try, and chased Dino down the stairs.

"Hold on for a minute," I said, making another grab for him. "You don't know that it was Henry J. who fired that shot at Sharon."

"The hell I don't. She knows about him, and he thinks she sicced us on to him. That's why he's been acting crazy. If Big Al found out he was selling a drug like that, she'd have his balls in a basket."

I had to agree that Big Al wouldn't like the competition, but Dino said that wasn't the problem.

"She'd kill him for exploiting women," he said.

"Exploiting women?" I said. "Dino, Big Al runs whores."

"It's not the same thing. Whores are in the game by choice. Ask Evelyn sometime."

As a matter of fact, I had asked Evelyn, and not so very long ago. She would have agreed with Dino, whatever the real truth was.

"You didn't know my uncles as well as I did, but you must remember they didn't touch dope, right?"

I remembered.

"Well, Big Al won't touch anything that exploits women. Topless dancers are OK. Whores are OK. But she draws the line at rough trade. Let anybody get out of line with one of her girls, and he's likely to find himself with a broken arm. Or leg. Or worse."

I was tired of standing out in the cold and arguing with him. Besides, he sounded as if he might know what he was talking about. It went along with one of my own theories.

"Look," I said, "I'll make a deal with you. We'll go talk to Henry J. That's all, though, just talk. No killing. Not even any beating. You didn't bring that baseball bat with you, by any chance?"

"No, damn it. I didn't even think about it. Did you bring anything?"

As a matter of fact, I'd brought the Mauser. It was stuck in the waistband of my pants, in the back, with my sweatshirt hanging down to cover it. I didn't see any point in telling Dino that, however.

So I changed the subject. "Where do you think Henry J. would be right now? At the Hurricane Club?"

"That's where I'd go if I'd just shot at somebody. Establish an alibi, just in case."

"Right. Any number of reliable witnesses at the Hurricane Club. The kind of guys the cops always believe without question."

Dino thought it over. "On the other hand, besides all those reliable witnesses, Big Al's usually there, too. It might not be the best place to go if you'd done something that she didn't know about and wouldn't approve of."

"Good thinking. I was hoping to try those enchiladas this time, though."

Dino shuddered. "Those things would kill you."

"I don't think so. We could find out."

"Not tonight. Henry J. wouldn't go there, not with Big Al around. I'll bet he's at home watching TV by now."

"We could drive by and see. If he's there, we could stop in for a little chat."

"And if he's not, we could go to the Hurricane Club."

"Sounds like a plan to me. Your car or mine?"

"You'd better drive," Dino said. "My hands are still shaking a little, just thinking about that son of a bitch."

BIG AL LIVED in one of the old nineteenth-century mansions on Avenue N, one that had been restored to more than a vestige of its former glory, but she didn't cohabit with Henry J. He lived alone in a house much less grand, not so very far from where I was staying.

It was an old ranch house on a couple of acres of land. The pastures that surrounded it belonged to someone else, but there were no cattle in them now. At the current price of cattle, no one but a millionaire could afford to be a rancher, and the millionaires were in it only for the tax losses.

"Does Henry J. think of himself as a gentleman rancher?" I asked.

"Henry J. doesn't think," Dino said. "What's a gentleman rancher, anyway?"

"A guy who wears clean boots," I said.

Dino didn't laugh, and I turned onto the oyster-shell road leading to Henry J.'s place, which squatted low and dark in front of us. There was only one light burning.

"What do we do, just go up and knock?" I said.

"Why not? Just old pals getting together. The son of a bitch."

I didn't think Dino had the right attitude about things, but at least he wasn't armed. Unless he'd lied to me, which wasn't impossible. After all, I'd lied to him.

When we got to the house, the truck's headlights showed that there was a black Ford Explorer in the garage.

"He's home," Dino said. "Good."

"You'll have to promise to behave yourself," I said. "Remember, we're just going to talk to him."

"I know it. You don't have to worry about me."

I hoped I could trust him, but I didn't really think I could. We got out of the truck and started toward the front door. I was walking behind Dino, and I nearly ran into him when he stopped suddenly.

"Did you hear that?" he asked.

"Hear what?"

"Sounded like a door slamming to me. I think the son of a bitch went out through the back. He must've heard us coming."

I hadn't made any special effort to keep quiet, and I hadn't turned off the headlights as we'd approached.

"I think you're hearing things," I said. "Besides, how would he know it's us?"

"He's got eyes, hasn't he? He might even have been expecting us."

"I don't think so. If he's really the one who shot at Sharon, he might think she's dead. She told me that she dropped to the floor after the shot. I don't think he's expecting anyone to show up."

"Why don't you go to the front door, and let me check the back," Dino said.

I was worried that Dino was trying to separate himself from me so he could try something with Henry J., if indeed Henry J. was anywhere around.

"I think we should stick together. You never know what we might run into."

"That's why we need to separate."

"If Henry J.'s really the one who took a shot at Sharon, he's got a gun."

It was most likely a handgun, I thought, since that would be easy to conceal. For all I knew, Henry J. had a permit that allowed him to carry a concealed handgun legally. It was now possible to get a permit like that in Texas if you were willing to take a class in handgun safety before getting the permit.

That's what I'd done, though it had worried me a little to take the class. Most of the other people in it looked as if they were just looking for an excuse to shoot someone. Come to think of it, Henry J. would probably have felt right at home.

"I'm not scared of Henry J.," Dino said, "gun or no gun. He's going to get away if we don't stop talking and do something. He can walk across one of those pastures to a road, and we'll never see him."

"He's not going to walk. He has a car here."

It was a pretty weak argument, and Dino wasn't persuaded. He didn't wait for me to say anything else. He just jogged away from me before I could get another word in.

I didn't know what else to do, so I went up to the front door and rang the bell.

There was no answer, but there was a noise in the back of the house. This time, I heard it.

It wasn't the sound of a door slamming.

It was the sound of a gunshot.

28

THE NEXT SOUND I heard was a yell that sounded a lot like it must have come from Dino. By that time I was running around the house. I pulled the Mauser out as I ran.

It was very dark in the backyard. There was no light from the house back there, and there were a couple of palm trees that shadowed the lawn. A dark shape lay in the shadows near one of the trees, and I dropped on one knee beside it.

"He shot me," Dino said, as if he were surprised. "The son of a bitch shot me."

"Where?" I asked.

"Right shoulder," Dino said, touching his shoulder.

I switched the Mauser to my left hand and put the right on Dino's shoulder. He flinched, but he didn't say anything. His shirt was wet, and I wiped my hand on the leg of my jeans.

"I'm OK," Dino said. "Go after him."

"Which way?"

Dino pointed off into the darkness. "Toward the road."

He didn't mean the road we'd come in on. There was another road parallel to it, and both of them led back to town.

"I'll be back in a minute," I said.

"Just don't let him shoot you."

I didn't intend to. I jogged across the yard, keeping as low as I could. At the rear of the yard there was a wooden fence, and I climbed over it. I wasn't presenting much of a target because the night was darker than the inside of a black cat, and I was wearing jeans and a navy blue sweatshirt.

On the other side of the fence, the weeds were high and thick and wet. My jeans were carrying five extra pounds by the time I'd gone twenty yards.

By that time it had occurred to me that I couldn't see anyone moving ahead of me. True, it was dark, but I should have been able to see *something* if anyone was out there.

I stopped and crouched down. There was no sign of a moon or stars, just a thick layer of black clouds that slid across the sky above me like a mile-long blackboard.

In the pasture there were a few bushes that stuck above the surrounding weeds, but they were just vague, dark shapes. Nothing was moving.

I could see the headlights of a car far down the road, coming in my direction. I waited as the lights got closer and closer, finally coming even with me and then going on past.

They didn't reveal anyone in precipitous flight, and they didn't show me anyone hiding in the bushes, but they did show me something else: a car that was parked on the shoulder of the road.

I couldn't tell what kind of car it was, but its presence opened up a couple of possibilities.

One was that the car just happened to have been abandoned in that particular spot. I didn't much believe in that kind of coincidence.

And if the car wasn't there by coincidence, a second possibility was that the shooter was skulking around one of those bushes ahead of me, waiting to take a shot at me before he made a run for the car.

The bushes were thick, with leaves still on them. Excellent places for skulking.

That led to a third possibility: that it wasn't Henry J. who'd shot Dino. It was someone else, someone who had what he, or, to be fair about it, she considered a legitimate reason for skulking around Henry J.'s house.

Whoever it was had a fine chance of getting to the car before I could do a thing about it. He was between me and the car, and he was carrying something that was either a pistol or a flashlight. I was willing to bet a Big Red that it wasn't a flashlight.

Of course, there was always a fourth possibility: that I could somehow sneak through the weeds, locate the shooter, and prevent him from getting to the car.

I could also win the Texas Lotto, though even the administrators of that little game had estimated that the chances of a person's winning it were roughly the same as a person's chances of getting attacked by a hammerhead shark on the streets of Lubbock at high noon in July. Or something like that. At any rate, the chances weren't good.

Still, I thought I had to do something, even if it was wrong, so I dropped to my belly and started inching my way along the ground. I might not be able to see anyone from that position, but no one could see me, either.

My idea was simply to head for the bush that was closest to the car. That was where I'd go if I were running from someone, which didn't really mean a thing, but it was at least a plan of action.

The ground was muddy, and I was getting as wet as I'd gotten in the previous day's rainstorm, but I wasn't going to stand up, not until I got close enough to the bush to have a decent shot at anyone hiding behind it.

It took me a while, but I finally got to within about twenty yards of the bush. I hoped I'd guessed right. If I hadn't, I was about to make a mistake that might get me killed. But it was certainly too late to worry about things if I was wrong.

I felt the ground around me and came up with a rock about the size of a regulation hardball. It was the oldest trick in the book, but it might work.

I came up to my knees and threw the rock to my right before ducking back down to wait for some kind of reaction—a rifle shot, the sound of running feet, anything.

I waited for at least a full minute. There was no reaction at all. Either I'd picked the wrong bush, or no one was anywhere around, or whoever was skulking there was too smart to fall for the oldest trick in the book.

I thought things over for a second or two. I didn't want to spend the night crouched in the mud, surrounded by wet weeds, and sooner or later I was going to have to take Dino to the hospital, so I had to do something.

Nothing had worked out so far, so I decided to do something really stupid.

I stood straight up and fired three rounds as fast as I could at the car parked on the road.

The car was too far for accurate shooting with a pistol, but I heard a kind of twanging sound, and I think I actually hit it once. Hitting it wasn't my real purpose, however. My purpose was to give the skulker something to worry about, not to mention some nice bright muzzle flashes to shoot at, with the hope that he wouldn't hit me.

If he didn't, then I'd know for sure where he was.

If he did, well, I'd still know where he was, though it most likely wouldn't do me much good.

I'd been right all along. He was behind the bush.

It took him just long enough to recover from his surprise at the shooting for me to fall back down in the mud. Almost before I hit the ground, he got off a return shot. It was a near thing, but he missed me. I imagined the bullet tunneling through the air exactly where my heart would have been if I'd remained standing.

Shooting scares me, especially if I'm the target and especially if the bullet comes close to me, close being defined as about a hundred yards, so I felt a little trembly in the stomach. I ignored the feeling, got to my knees, and triggered off two shots at his muzzle flash. The shooter was thinking fast, however, and he'd started to run as soon as he'd fired. I missed by a mile.

He wasn't going to shoot again. He was in an all-out run for the car, so I jumped up and went after him.

He was faster than I was, and more agile. I didn't know whether he could see better than I could, but he'd somehow avoided the hole I stepped in. It wasn't a big hole, but it was big enough to swallow my entire foot.

I fell, sprawling, and the Mauser flew out of my hand.

I was up soon enough, but I fell right back down, having not only stepped in a hole but having managed to twist my bad knee in the process. It felt as if someone were doing surgery on it with a red-hot crowbar. Tears came into my eyes, and I bit down on my lip to keep from yelling.

There was a kind of roaring in my head, but not so loud that I couldn't hear the car starting, and then I could hear it backing and turning to make a U-ey before it drove away.

I didn't try to go after it. I just sat there for a while, waiting for the pain to lessen.

I don't know how long it took, maybe five minutes, maybe more. I tried standing up without putting too much pressure on the knee. It was going to be OK. It didn't feel any worse than it would have if someone had been hitting it with the rounded part of a ball peen hammer every time I took a step.

I looked around for the Mauser, found it a few feet from where I'd fallen, and picked it up. I wiped it off on my sweatshirt as best I could and stuck it back in my waistband.

Then I started back toward the house to see how Dino was.

HE WAS SITTING with his back against the palm tree when I walked up to him.

"I knew it was you when you came over the fence," he said. "You're a really graceful guy, you know that?"

I'd been about as graceful as a cat. A cat with its tail and three of its legs in splints, that is.

"Did you get that bastard?" Dino asked.

"No. He had a car parked over there on the road. He got away."

"Get a look at him?"

I'd gotten a look, but all I'd seen was a bulky blur.

"It was someone big," I said. "Or maybe just tall. That's about all I could tell you."

"I heard shooting. Was that you or him?"

"Both," I said.

"Did you hit him?"

"I don't think so."

"Too bad." Dino stood up, bracing himself on the tree bole. "I thought you said you didn't have a gun."

"I lied."

"I figured that out."

"How bad's your shoulder?"

"Judging from the way you were walking, it's probably not as bad as your knee. What happened?"

"I stepped in a hole and fell down."

"Like I said, a really graceful guy. Oh, well. Falling down's better than being shot, I guess."

"I think so," I said. "You feel like walking to the house now?"

"You don't think that was Henry J. out there in the pasture?"

"Do you?"

"Nah. He wouldn't have had a car waiting. I don't think Henry J.'s gonna be in the house, though."

I didn't agree. I was afraid Henry J. was going to be there, all right. Dino was, too. He just didn't want to say what he really meant.

We walked to the house, or rather, I hobbled, and Dino sort of shuffled. We were quite a pair.

The back door was open, just as I'd thought it would be. I turned on a light that revealed us as standing in the kitchen. It was very clean and didn't look as if it got much use.

We went through the kitchen into the den, where the light was already on, and that's where we found Henry J.

He was lying in the middle of the brown rug, and there was a dark stain underneath him.

I limped over to the window, tracking mud all the way. Henry J. wouldn't mind.

The window wasn't shattered like the one in Sharon's door, but there was a neat, round hole in it, three thin cracks spreading out from its edges.

"Stay here for a second," I told Dino and went back into the kitchen to check the back door.

The lock had been shot off. I thought that Henry J. had been shot from outside, and then the killer had come inside to make sure of him.

The situation with Sharon had been different. She lived in a crowded part of town, and someone might have happened on the scene at any moment. Checking on her would have been too big a risk. For all the killer knew, unless he knew her well, she might even have been dialing 911.

I went back to where Dino was standing, looking down at the body. He touched it with his toe.

"I never much liked Henry J.," he said. "I even thought he tried to kill Sharon. So why do I feel sorry for him now?"

I felt the same way, but it wasn't anything I could explain. It's just a lot easier for most of us to dislike a living person than a dead one.

"Do you think the same person who shot at Sharon killed Henry J.?" Dino asked.

"Yeah. It would be too much of a coincidence for it to be any other way."

"So where does that leave us?"

I wasn't sure. It shot the hell out of one of my earlier theories, however. I was beginning to develop a new theory, but I wasn't quite ready to put it into words.

So I said, "We have to call the police."

Dino frowned. "I had a feeling you were going to say that," he said.

29

HE TRIED TO talk me out of it, but we didn't argue for very long. Even Dino knew that this time we had to call the cops. The surprise was who they sent along with the evidence team: Bob Lattner. He wasn't exactly the person I wanted most to see.

He wasn't pleased to see me, either, especially not with the body of Henry J. on the floor between us.

"Why'd you and Dino kill him, Smith?" Lattner asked casually, as if he were asking what we'd had for breakfast.

Dino looked at me as if to say, See what comes from calling the cops?

"We didn't kill anyone," I told Lattner. "We came here to talk to Henry J., and we found him lying on the floor right here."

"You got any proof of that?"

"There was someone else here when we got here. We chased him, and he shot Dino in the shoulder. You should save the questioning and let the paramedics have a look at Dino now."

I'd called for an ambulance as soon as I'd called the police, and the paramedics were waiting right outside. Lattner wouldn't let them come in. He didn't want his crime scene disturbed.

"Don't worry," he said. "He'll get treatment in a little while."

"I think he needs it now," I said.

Lattner started to say something, changed his mind, and said, "You're right. Go on, Dino, but don't try to leave the premises."

Dino didn't say a word. He brushed by Lattner and went outside to the ambulance.

Lattner and I moved to the side of the room while the evidence team took pictures, dusted for prints, drew diagrams, and began poking at Henry J.'s body.

"Tell me about it," Lattner said, and I did.

I even told him the part about Sharon. His mouth got tight when I reached the part about the GHB, but he didn't interrupt me.

"Why didn't you call us about the shooting?" he asked when I was finished.

"You know Dino," I said. "He doesn't like to deal with the police if he doesn't have to."

Lattner turned his back on me for a minute, watching the evidence team at work. When he turned back, he said, "He likes to handle things himself, right? So the two of you came out here and took care of things."

"That's ridiculous," I said. "Besides, you don't believe it. So why don't you just drop it?"

That didn't make him like me any better. He said, "Do you remember what I told you the other day in the drugstore, Smith?"

"I'm not sure I know what you're talking about," I said, though I was.

"I told you not to mess around in things that didn't concern you. I told you that if you fooled around in a case I was working on, I was really going to get pissed off."

"Oh," I said. "That. So you're trying to get me to confess to a murder I didn't commit just because I piss you off?"

"You see?" Lattner said. "That's one of the things I don't like about you, Smith, that smart-ass attitude of yours. This time it's going to get you in real trouble. Because I happen to know you have a motive for killing Henry J."

"I have a motive?" I said. This time, I had no idea what he was talking about.

"That's right. A motive. You and Henry J. had quite a little ruckus last night, and your buddy Dino was in on it, too. And tonight Henry J. tried to get a little revenge on the two of you by scaring Dino's daughter. So you came out here tonight to finish things. Well, you finished them, all right."

It actually made a kind of sense. If I'd been in Lattner's position, I might even have believed it myself. But I wasn't in Lattner's position.

"There was someone else here," I said, and before he could contradict me I went on. "Otherwise, how do you explain the wound in Dino's shoulder? Henry J. doesn't have a pistol on him, so he didn't do it."

Lattner gave me an up-and-down look. "You look like you've been dragged through a swamp. So you went out and hid the pistol in the weeds. We'll find it."

"No you won't. And Henry J. wasn't shot with my pistol, either. So where does that leave you?"

"It leaves me still ready to hang your ass, Smith."

It was time to get off that topic. I thought I might tell him one of my new theories. I had a feeling it would take his mind off me for a while.

"You didn't tell me that you were Kelly Davis's uncle," I said. "If anyone had a motive to kill Henry J., it was you."

Something red flared deep in his eyes, and I thought for just a second that he was going to hit me. But he must have realized that there were too many witnesses for him to be able to get away with it.

So he settled for calling me a ten-letter word. I was surprised he knew one that long.

"Henry J. was selling GHB to some of the kids at that party Kelly went to," I said. "You've been working on Randall Kirbo's disappearance a lot longer than I have, and you don't have a very high opinion of my investigative abilities, so you should have found out about the GHB as easily as I did. What if Henry J. sold something like that to a kid who slipped it in Kelly's drink? What would you do to Henry J.?"

He didn't answer, but then he didn't have to. The answer was easy enough to read on his face.

"And if Randall Kirbo was the kid who slipped the GHB in the drink," I said, "what would you do to him? Plant him in a sand dune somewhere?"

"Shut up," Lattner said. His voice sounded as if someone were squeezing his neck with both hands. "Don't say another word, Smith."

He didn't scare me, not with all those witnesses around. They were going about their business with great concentration, but I was sure they'd notice if he tried to kill me.

At least I hoped they would.

"GHB can kill people," I went on. "It's cheap, and it's easy to make. A capful costs, what? Ten dollars? Henry J. was probably selling it for twenty. It doesn't take much to knock a person out, and it can even affect some people by making them so sleepy that they don't ever wake up. Is that what happened to Kelly?"

"You can walk out of here tonight, Smith," Lattner said. "But someday I'll catch you when there's no one around to look out for you. Then you'll be sorry you didn't shut your mouth when I told you to."

"Maybe. But I'm going to finish what I'm saying. GHB can't be detected by the routine drug screen at an autopsy. Kelly could have been full of it, and no one would have known. Is that it? Is that what happened?"

He squeezed the words out. "How . . . the . . . hell . . . would . . . I . . . know?"

"I just have the feeling that you would, being the ace investigator that you are. If a pud like me can figure it out, surely you could."

"You'd better leave now, Smith. It might be your last chance."

"Fine with me. I thought you were going to arrest me and throw me under the jail."

"Like you said, all the evidence points to the fact that someone else was here tonight. But you'll be questioned again. Hold yourself available."

"Sure," I said. I started for the door.

"And Smith," he called after me.

"What?"

"No matter how smart you think you are, you don't have any idea what's really going on. Before this is over, you're going to screw everything up. And then I'm going to nail you."

I didn't let it bother me. After all, he was probably right.

30

DINO WAS LOOKING less than dapper in a cast that the paramedics had rigged on him, but aside from that, he didn't look especially bothered by the fact that he'd been recently shot in the shoulder.

"What did they give you?" I asked.

"Some kind of hypo. I don't like needles, but whatever was in the one they just stuck me with is OK by me. They took ten stitches, and I didn't feel a one of them."

"Good. Are you ready to get out of here?"

"Hell, yes. I'm the one who wanted to go before the cops came, remember?"

"Was that you? I thought it was me."

"Don't kid around. I'm leaving right now."

It sounded like a good idea to me, so we jumped into the S-10 and took off. Well, "jumped" isn't an exact description of what we did, but we got in without falling down and humiliating ourselves.

We drove back toward Galveston, coming in behind the seawall on Stewart Road because it was quicker to get to Dino's house that way. I had the radio tuned to the oldies station, and we were listening to "Take a Chance on Me" by ABBA, the only group from the disco era that I thought was worth hearing. Well, not counting the Village People.

"You didn't get a look at who shot you, by any chance?" I said.

"Nope. Too dark, and too far away. You got a better look at him than I did."

He was right, and I hadn't seen much in the darkness. It could have been almost anyone.

"Do you think it could have been Lattner?" I asked.

Dino sat up a little straighter in the seat, wincing when a pain shot through his shoulder. He might not have felt the stitches when they went in, but he was feeling them now. The shot was probably wearing off.

I was feeling my knee, too, but at least I was able to drive. There've been times when I couldn't even do that much.

"Lattner?" Dino said. "What makes you ask a thing like that?"

"I was just wondering how he got there so fast."

"You noticed that, huh?"

I'd noticed, all right. Lattner had arrived on the scene before anyone else, almost as if he'd been waiting for the call. Or as if he'd been in the neighborhood.

"It might not mean anything," I said.

"Then again, it might," Dino said. "But there's something else I've been thinking about."

ABBA was replaced by Roy Orbison. "Pretty Woman," of course.

"Eventually they're going to wear that one out," Dino said. "And then they'll have to play 'In Dreams.' Or maybe even 'Only the Lonely.' "

I didn't have the heart to tell him that CDs didn't wear out. And even if they did, the station would probably just buy another copy of "Pretty Woman."

"You were going to tell me what you'd been thinking about," I said.

"Oh, yeah. I know it sounds crazy, but what if the person who shot at Sharon and the person who killed Henry J. *were* two different people? It's possible, isn't it?"

I didn't think so. I still liked Lattner for both jobs, but I thought I'd go along with Dino this time just to hear what he had to say. He likes to be humored now and then.

"It's possible," I said. "Not very likely, but possible. Why?"

He squirmed a little, trying to get comfortable. I could have told him that he wasn't going to be comfortable for several days, not with a little chunk of his shoulder shot out, but he'd figure it out for himself sooner or later, if he hadn't already.

"This is the way I figure it," he said. "Sharon knew that Henry J. was selling GHB at the party at Big Al's beach house, but since she hadn't told anyone, he didn't think he had to do anything about it. Then you and I started nosing around. If it had been just you, he might not have thought of Sharon, but when I showed up, he thought she'd dropped the dime on him."

"It costs a quarter to make a phone call now," I said. "Unless you've got one of those phone cards that everybody's selling."

"You really are a flippant bastard, aren't you?"

"True, but I'm good for your vocabulary."

"I'm serious about this, Tru. What's wrong with what I said?"

"Nothing. Go on and tell me the rest of it."

"I'm not sure I want to."

"It's either that or listen to Gerry and the Pacemakers," I said as "Ferry Cross the Mersey" came on the radio.

"Jesus, what a bunch of wimps," Dino said, reaching out to snap off the radio. "Don't they every play the Stones?"

"About once a month, I imagine. And they never play 'Sympathy for the Devil.'"

"It figures. Anyway, what I was thinking was that maybe Big Al found out about what Henry J. was up to. Maybe he got worried about shooting at Sharon and even went by and told Big Al about it. She told him to go home, simmered for a few minutes, and then went out there and shot him. It could have happened that way, couldn't it?"

It could have, but I didn't think it had. I told Dino that there was one way to find out, though.

"How's that?" Dino said.

"We can go and ask her," I said.

31

I WASN'T REALLY sure that another visit to the Hurricane Club was a good idea, considering the fact that neither Dino nor I was in what you could call prime condition, but Dino assured me that he could take anything Big Al could dish out, and although I didn't believe it for a second, I was too macho to admit that I wasn't so sure about myself.

Anyway, this time I had my pistol. And the bartender didn't have his little baseball bat. He'd had the one we took away from him for forty years, so I didn't expect him to replace it anytime soon.

So we drove up to the club again and parked practically in the same spot we'd used the night before. I wondered if that was a good omen or a bad one.

Dino didn't seem to care. He got out of the truck with surprising ease, and he was practically inside the club before I was able to catch up with him.

"Don't be in such a hurry," I told him. "I'm sure they have enough enchiladas for both of us."

"I'm not interested in ordering dinner," he said. "I think we're on the right track here."

I didn't, but it was nice to see him so enthusiastic about something besides a bargain on the Home Shopping Network for a change. Maybe I should consider making him a partner. That way, we'd both get out of the house a lot more often.

The inside of the Hurricane Club was no more appealing than it had been on our previous visit, maybe even less so, and the clientele looked pretty much the same, except that the guy with the eye patch was missing.

The Christmas tree on the bar didn't look any worse, as far as I could see, but it might have shed a few more of its needles. I suspected that by New Year's Eve there would be a pile of brown needles about an inch deep under it, while the branches of the tree would be completely bare.

The jukebox was playing a seasonal number, a syrupy instrumental version of "White Christmas" that would have driven away any self-respecting tough guy. It was almost bad enough to make *me* want to turn around and go back outside.

Big Al was sitting alone at her table. There was no food in front of her this time; she'd most likely eaten already. She took a drink from a beer bottle, but she set it on the table when we came in and motioned for us to join her.

"Don't worry," she said when we got to the table. "I'm not the type to hold grudges. What happened last night was partly my fault, after all. Sometimes I think I should keep Henry J. on a tighter leash."

She didn't know the half of it, or I didn't think she did. If Dino was right, however, she was way ahead of me. And she was also a damned good actress.

"Willie won't bother you, either," she said. "In case you were wondering."

Willie must have been the bartender. I glanced over in his direction, but he was ignoring us completely, polishing a spot on the bar with great concentration. It was probably the only spot on the bar that had been polished within the last quarter of a century.

Dino sat down and said, "We weren't worried about Willie. We can handle him."

Big Al looked pointedly at his arm and gave me the old up and down.

"The two of you don't look like you could handle a three-year-old girl with the flu. You look like somebody dragged you through Offatt's Bayou about an inch off the bottom, Smith. What happened to you two, anyway?"

"You should know," Dino said.

It came out hard and flat, sort of like Jack Webb might have said it on *Dragnet*. I thought again that I should hire Dino. He was a lot better at this than I was. Of course, I was pretty sure that he was on the wrong track, but that didn't bother me. The thing was that he *sounded* as if he were absolutely right.

I was still standing, and Big Al looked up at me quizzically.

"Do you have any idea what he's talking about?" she asked.

I nodded. "I'm afraid so."

"I wish you'd let me in on it, then."

I was about to, but in the pause between the end of "White Christmas" and the beginning of Tony Bennett's "I Left My Heart in San Francisco," I heard the phone ring at the end of the bar. Willie went over to answer it, and I had a sudden premonition that I knew what the call was about.

"Something's happened," I said. "Something that I think we need to talk over."

"She knows what's happened," Dino said. "She's the one behind it."

Willie was walking over to the table. He looked like a man who had just lost five grand at the dog track and didn't know how he was going to explain it to his wife.

"The phone's for you," he told Big Al.

She made no move to get up. "Who is it? Can't you take a message?"

Willie looked at me and Dino. "You'd better just take it yourself," he said.

Big Al pushed back her chair and got up. She knew better than to press Willie for details. You never knew who might be calling. It could be someone she didn't want Dino and me to know about, like her snitch in the police department. I didn't doubt that she had one. I was just surprised that it had taken him this long to call, if that was who it was.

While Big Al was walking toward the phone, Dino turned to me and said, "You're not playing this right. If you wanna do the good cop, bad cop routine, that's OK, but you gotta work with me a little better."

"I don't want to do any routine," I said. "I don't think Big Al has any idea about what's happened tonight. If I'm right, that's someone calling to tell her right now."

"How could you know that?"

"I don't know it. But judging from the way Willie the Bartender looked, it has to be bad news. Can you think of any other really bad news that Big Al might be getting right about now?"

He couldn't, but he hated to admit it. We both looked at Big Al as she talked into the telephone receiver. After a while she hung it up and stood where she was, looking out over the room. I don't think she was seeing anything, however.

After what seemed like quite a while, she reached out and grabbed the handle of a nearly empty beer mug that was sitting on the bar. She threw the mug as hard as she could at the Christmas tree, which exploded into a shower of needles and sparkly ornaments.

The tree didn't do much to slow down the mug, which kept right on going, past the end of the bar, crashing through the front of the jukebox and cutting off the Four Aces right in the middle of "Three Coins in the Fountain." By the time most of the lights in the jukebox had blinked out, the clientele of the Hurricane Club had faded silently away. They might not have known what was going on, but they knew they didn't want to be part of it. The only people left in the place were Dino, me, Big Al, and Willie, who was studiously ignoring the rest of us. He'd already lost his baseball bat, and he wasn't going to lose anything else.

Big Al came back over to the table, reached out one big hand, and grabbed Dino's shoulder. His face turned red, and his eyes bugged out, but he didn't fall out of the chair. She squeezed a little harder. Dino listed sharply to the right, but he still didn't make a sound.

Big Al wasn't looking at Dino while she squeezed. She was looking at me, and not with affection.

"You sons of bitches," she said. "I ought to kill both of you right here."

"We didn't do anything to Henry J.," I said. "We're just the ones who found him."

"That's not what I heard."

"Well, you heard wrong. Let go of Dino's shoulder, and I'll tell you what happened."

She didn't move her hand, but she let up on the pressure a bit. Dino sagged in the chair and took a deep, shuddering breath.

"Why should I believe a damn word you say?" Big Al asked.

"Because it'll be the truth. Would we have come here if we'd killed Henry J.? We may be stupid, but we're not entirely crazy."

"Maybe not." Big Al didn't sound completely convinced, though she took her hand away from Dino. "But if I ever find out that you had anything to do with killing Henry J., you'll be feeding the crabs in about ten minutes."

I didn't much like the idea of becoming crab fodder, but I said, "Fair enough. Now do you want to hear what really happened, or not?"

She wanted to hear. She sat down across from Dino, who was still in no condition to join in the conversation. I sat beside her and told her about Sharon and about what had happened when we got to Henry J.'s place.

"And you think he'd shoot at her because of some little thing like that GHB?" Big Al said when I was finished.

"Why not?" I said. "Henry J. wasn't exactly shy about hurting people, and Sharon knew something that could get him in big trouble if she told it."

"In the first place, who's she gonna tell? The cops? They wouldn't believe her, and if they did, they couldn't prove anything."

"What if she told you?"

"I already knew. I found out about it months ago, and I straightened Henry J. out, believe me. He and I understood each other, and all it took was a little discussion."

Big Al paused and her eyes misted up; she squeezed them shut. I couldn't believe what I was seeing. Tears started to run down her cheeks, beside her nose.

"Henry J. was the only friend I ever had," she said, opening her eyes and wiping her face with the back of her hand. "He was the only man I ever trusted. And you think *I* killed him? You're crazy, all right."

I would have told her that it was all Dino's idea, but this didn't seem to be the right time for that. Dino might have spoken up himself, but he still wasn't talking.

"I'm sorry," I said. "I'm going to find whoever did it, though. You can count on it."

Big Al sniffed and pulled a paper napkin from the black metal holder that sat on the table. She dried her eyes and tossed the wadded napkin on the table.

"Maybe you're going to find him, and maybe you're not," she said.

Her eyes were still sparkling, but they were as hard as the head of a railroad spike.

"Why do you say that?"

"Maybe I'll find him first. If I do, there won't be anything left for you to find."

I could tell she wasn't joking, but I wasn't too worried. I didn't think she was going to find anyone.

I turned to Dino. "Are you about ready to leave, or would you like a beer?"

"Uh," Dino said.

I didn't think this would be a good time to remind him that he'd told me he could take anything Big Al could dish out. I put a hand under his elbow and helped him to his feet. We looked like two very old men as we hobbled toward the door.

I looked over at Willie, but he wasn't interested in trying anything, which was just as well. I don't think Dino and I could have handled him. For that matter, I don't think we could have handled Minnie Mouse.

"You two'd better go home and go to bed," Big Al said to our backs.

I didn't see any point in arguing with her. It was probably the best idea I'd heard all night.

32

DINO HAD A little more trouble getting in the truck this time, but after a little maneuvering, I got him into a sitting position and fastened the seat belt around him.

I was about to shut the door when he said, "You took your pistol in there, didn't you?"

I admitted that I had.

"Why didn't you shoot her, then?"

"What would I have told Lattner? That Big Al squeezed you a little too hard?"

"I wish I had a pistol," Dino said. "I'd use it to shoot *you.*"

He was only kidding, though. I think.

We were almost to his house before he said anything else, and it wasn't anything that I'd expected.

"Was Big Al really crying?" he asked.

"I think so. It surprised me, too."

"Yeah. I would have bet she couldn't do it. She really must have liked old Henry J."

"Two hearts beating as one," I said.

"I don't think that was it, exactly," Dino said. "I think they understood each other, but that's about all."

I stopped the S-10 in front of his house and walked around to help him out.

"I can make it just fine," he said, pushing away the hand I offered.

"I know that. I was just making sure."

"Yeah. I believe that like I believe Big Al didn't really want to hurt me."

He got out without my help, but it took him a while. When he had both feet planted on the ground, I said, "You don't still think Big Al shot Henry J., do you?"

"Hell, no. That was no act we saw back there. I thought she was going to kill me, but there was nothing personal in it. I was just there for her to take it out on."

"And you don't hold it against her?"

"If it hadn't been for me," he said, "we wouldn't have been at the Hurricane Club. Besides, I don't blame her. I was handy, and she needed to hurt somebody. I might have done the same thing in her place."

"No, you wouldn't. Your uncles, maybe, but not you."

"Yeah, well, you never know."

That was true. You never really know about anyone, no matter how well you might think you know them.

We started slowly up the walk to Dino's front door. He was walking a lot better now than he'd been back at Big Al's place. So was I, for that matter. In a week or so, we'd be as good as new. Or so I liked to tell myself.

Dino opened his door and said, "If Big Al didn't kill Henry J. and take a shot at Sharon, who did? Lattner?"

"I wouldn't put it past him. He's mixed up in things some way or another. But I have some other ideas, too."

"Are you going to tell me what they are?"

"I may have done too much of that already."

"Now what the hell does that mean?" Dino asked.

"Do you feel like hearing it?"

"Not out here. Come on in."

We went inside. Dino sat on his couch and reached for his remote control. I beat him to it and pushed it aside.

"If I'm going to talk, I'm not going to compete with some screaming cretin on that TV set."

"Cretin?"

"You could look it up."

"Right. And then I have to use it in a sentence. Like 'flippant.'"

"You did real well with that one."

"Yeah. Now tell me about those ideas of yours. Or better yet, don't tell me. Not yet. I'm going to take a bunch of aspirin right now."

He got off the couch under his own power and shuffled off to find the aspirin. I sat in a chair near the coffee table and waited for him to come back. When he did, he didn't look any better, but then it takes a while for aspirin to do any good. He sat back on the couch and looked at me.

"About those ideas of yours," he said.

"I don't have a lot of ideas," I told him, "but I do have a couple of questions."

"Questions? What about?"

"About your old college pal Tack Kirbo."

"Tack? What about him?"

"Is he still in town?" I asked.

It was something I should have thought of sooner, but it hadn't really occurred to me. When I look for people these days, I don't give formal reports to my clients, and I'd simply assumed that the Kirbos had gone back home to wait for some word on what I'd found out. Dino had guaranteed my fee, and there was no reason for the Kirbos to stick around.

But, as it turned out, they had.

"Sure they're here," Dino told me. "They're right there at the Galvez."

"I had a feeling you were going to say that. And because you did, I have another question. Have you been talking to them?"

"Them?"

"Don't get legalistic on me, Dino. You know what I mean."

"Yeah, I guess I do."

He looked hopefully at the remote control. I picked it up and held it in my hand.

"I'll let you have this just as soon as you answer the question."

"OK, OK. I've talked to Tack a couple of times. He's an old friend, after all."

"So what did you talk about?"

"Nothing much. Just about how we were looking into things and that we'd run down a couple of leads."

" 'We,' " I said. "You told him 'we.' "

Dino tried to look innocent. He wasn't very good at it, however.

"Sure I did. We were working together part of the time, weren't we?"

"And so you told him about Big Al and Henry J."

"Why not? You don't think Tack had anything to do with all this, do you?"

"It's not impossible. You couldn't have told him about Sharon, though, since we didn't know anything about that part of things."

"Well . . ."

"Well, what? Oh, hell." I'd forgotten for a second that he'd known all along that Sharon had been at the party. "You don't mean you told him that she was at the beach house."

"It might have come up while we were talking."

"Either you told him or you didn't. Which is it?"

"OK, I told him. I didn't see any reason not to."

I couldn't really blame him. I don't think I would have seen any reason not to, either.

"Kirbo might know more than we think he does about the whole mess," I said. "He might even have had someone else working on this, for all we know. And he might even have a reason for blaming Sharon for what happened to his son, now that he knows she was at the party."

Dino rubbed his face. He looked a little ragged around the edges, and whatever good the shot had done him at first, Big Al's grip on his shoulder had canceled it out.

"You don't really believe that, do you? That Tack would try to kill Sharon, I mean."

"You know him better than I do," I said. "He's your old pal."

He thought about it for a minute and came to a conclusion he didn't really want to put into words. He finally made himself do it, however.

"I think he might have done it if he was mad enough," he said.

33

IT WAS NEARLY eleven o'clock by the time I got to the Galvez. The Christmas tree was still in the lobby, but the bell ringers were gone, back to wherever they'd come from with happy memories of the holiday season in festive Galveston.

I wasn't feeling festive at all, and I was afraid that the Kirbos wouldn't be going home with pleasant memories. When I called their room on the house phone, Janey Kirbo answered on the first ring.

I asked her if I could talk to her and her husband, but she said that might not be a good idea. She asked if she could meet me in the lobby.

"Sure," I told her. "I'll be on one of those couches in the front hall, looking out at the Gulf."

I couldn't really see the Gulf, but I sat on the couch anyway. She arrived in about five minutes, which surprised me a little. I thought people in Lubbock were the early-to-bed type, so I'd assumed she'd need a little time to get dressed.

She looked tired. There were circles under her eyes, and her makeup could have used a refresher. She sank to the couch and sighed.

"Trouble?" I said.

"No more than usual. What did you want to talk to us about?"

"I really wanted to talk to your husband," I said. "I had a few questions to ask him."

"Anything you could ask him, you can ask me. I'm sure I can answer for him."

"I don't doubt that. Where is he, by the way?"

"Do you really want to know?"

I told her that I really did.

"All right. I hate to burden you with dirty little family secrets, but he's up in the room, passed out on the bed. Fully clothed, of course, and snoring very loudly."

"He had a hard day, I take it," I said, thinking that all that shooting and running away had tired him out.

"It was no harder than any other day that he has. He's not asleep, Mr. Smith. He's passed out drunk."

I didn't know what to say to that, since it didn't exactly fit with my expectations. So I didn't say anything at all, a tactic that's often proved useful in the past. Sometimes other people will talk just to fill the vacuum. That's what Janey Kirbo did.

"When you met us the other day," she said, "you must have noticed how much Tack liked his liquor."

I nodded. "Lots of people do."

"With him, it's more than just liking. It's an illness. He's an alcoholic, but of course he won't admit it. I've tried talking to him, but he insists that his drinking isn't a problem. He says he has it under control."

"That's what he said about Randall, too."

"Well, he's wrong. About himself, and about our son. Randall was well on his way to becoming an alcoholic, too, if he wasn't one already."

"That's not what—"

She didn't give me a chance to finish the sentence.

"I know that's not what Tack said the other day. But it's the truth. Tack has been lying to himself for so long, he almost believes he's telling the truth. But I know better. So does he, somewhere deep down. That just makes it harder, for both of us."

I remembered how she'd looked the day I met her. I'd wondered then if there wasn't more to the story of Randall's disappearance than I was getting. Now I knew that there was, and she was going to tell me about it.

"I'm never going to see my son again, am I, Mr. Smith?" she asked.

I didn't much want to tell her what I really thought, but I didn't think this was the time to lie to her.

"I'm afraid not," I said. "I'm pretty sure something's happened to him. Something bad."

"I'm sure, too. I've been sure from the beginning, but there was no way I could convince Tack of that. He kept telling me that Randall was a mature and responsible adult, that he knew how to handle himself, that he could control any situation he found himself in. Maybe Tack believes that, along with everything else he believes. But then he thinks *he's* a mature and responsible adult. That should tell you something."

It told me something, all right. I wasn't sure just what, however.

"So all that about Randall drinking maybe a little but certainly not a lot, all that was a lie."

She smiled. It wasn't much of a smile, but at least it was a try.

"Let's call it an exaggeration," she said. "An exaggeration by an overindulgent parent."

"Whatever we call it, Randall was probably drunk at that party," I said.

"I would say so. But he didn't get drunk in front of Tack, of course."

"Of course," I said, though if he had it might have made a difference. It was far too late to worry about that now, however.

"So I guess there's no chance your husband came down here to the Island during spring break to check up on your son," I said.

"No chance at all. Why check up on someone you knew was behaving in a mature and responsible way?"

She had a point there.

"There's just one other thing," I said. "Have you been with your husband all evening?"

"No. I rarely am. For some reason, he doesn't seem to want my company when he's getting drunk. For most of the evening he was most likely doing what he does best, entertaining whatever two or three men he could find in the bar who would listen to his stories about the good old days, when men were football players, when there was, by God, a Southwest Conference, and when quarterbacks could take a hit without crying to the ref. When God was in his heaven and all was right with the world."

"But you weren't with him while he entertained those two or three men."

"No. I was in our room, reading a book. Do you read, Mr. Smith?"

I admitted that I did, occasionally, read a book. I could have told her a little bit about John O'Hara, but she wasn't really interested in a literary discussion.

"I read a lot of books," she said. "I find that it helps."

I knew what she meant. I thanked her for talking to me and told her that I'd call when I found out anything more about her son.

She stood up. "Why were you so interested in Tack's whereabouts?" she asked.

"Someone got shot tonight. I thought maybe Tack had a hand in it."

She smiled wistfully, almost as if she wished he'd been involved.

"Tack isn't a man of action," she said. "More a man of words." Another smile, so brief that I could have been imagining it. "Most of them slurred."

I thanked her again, and she went back to her room. Her shoulders were slumped when she began to walk away from me down the hall, but they were squared again before she'd gone ten feet.

34

BEFORE I LEFT the hotel I went by to have a brief chat with the bartender, a young man who resembled Willie no more than the bar in the Galvez resembled the one in the Hurricane Club. He looked more like a moonlighting Eagle Scout. And he remembered Tack Kirbo, all right.

"He's a nice enough guy," he said. "Comes in every night and drinks too much, talking about football to anybody who'll listen to him."

"You let him drink too much?"

"I try to cut him off before he gets too far gone. He's not driving, and he always walks out in a straight line. I'd say he keeps a bottle in his room, though. Lots of guys like that do."

I didn't doubt it. I left the bar and went outside, where a cold wind was blowing, sliding under my sweatshirt and chilling me to the bone.

I got in the truck, started the motor, and turned on the heater. I knew just about everything I needed to know now, or at least I had all the pieces. I didn't know how they fit together, but I thought I could get them into some kind of order if I thought about it long enough. I should have figured it out earlier, but it would have been easier if everyone had been honest with me.

There was just one big problem remaining. If I was able to figure things out, someone else could do it, too. And someone else had a slightly different idea about how justice should be done.

It was awfully late, but I was sure the Hurricane Club would still be open. I thought I might as well drive by and see if Big Al was still there.

SHE WASN'T AT her table. There were only three customers, and Willie. I walked over to the bar, little pieces of Christmas ornaments crunching under my shoes. I was sure they'd still be there next Christmas, crushed so fine that they'd become part of the sawdust.

Willie was looking at a glass he was drying, and he didn't look up at me when I stood in front of the bar. I waited for a few seconds but he was really interested in that glass. So I said, "I need to see Big Al."

"She's not here," he said.

"I'll just drop by her house, then," I said.

Willie stuck the glass under the bar and located another one to dry. It didn't even look wet.

"You do that," he said.

I DIDN'T GO by Big Al's house because I was certain she wouldn't be there. What I did do was stop at a convenience store and call the police station to ask for Bob Lattner. He wasn't there, which didn't surprise me.

"I need to talk to him," I told the dispatcher. "It's about the shooting tonight."

The dispatcher was really sorry, but he couldn't get in touch with Lattner. That didn't surprise me, either. I said thanks and hung up.

INTERSTATE 45 BETWEEN Houston and Galveston is never quiet. Even after midnight, the cars stream up and down it, all of them going somewhere, I suppose, though I have no idea where. What business could all those people possibly have in Galveston at that time of night? Or even in Houston, for that matter. I knew what I was doing there, but surely all those other cars weren't filled with valiant investigators bent on preventing crime. Whatever their business was, they were all in a hurry, as usual, and this time, so was I.

I could see the Union Carbide plant from the interstate, its thousands of twinkling lights in perfect harmony with the season, but this time I wasn't stopping in Texas City. It was probably already too late to help Patrick Mullen.

The way I had things figured, Chad Peavy was the key to everything. His behavior should have been a clue, but I'd been so sure that he'd been threatened by Henry J. that I attributed his actions to his fear. He'd been afraid, all right, but not of Henry J. Or at least not for the reasons I'd thought.

Chad had told me that he and Randall Kirbo had driven out to the beach house together. If Randall hadn't come home from the party, Chad would have known about it.

And Chad was the one who'd told me about Sharon when I'd led him to believe there was another witness. He had to be the one who'd taken a shot at her, and the one who'd killed Henry J. He'd probably killed Randall Kirbo, too, but I wasn't sure about that.

And I wasn't sure just why he'd done any of the other things, though I thought I had at least some of the answers.

Big Al had some of the answers, too. She'd known that Henry J. had been tailing me, so she must have known where we'd gone. She might even have known why Chad would have a reason to go gunning for Henry J. In fact, I was pretty sure that she did.

Hadn't she told me that she knew about Henry J.'s drug activities and that she'd straightened him out? If she knew about the drugs, she might very well have known everything that had happened at her beach house that night. She might even have been blackmailing Chad Peavy. It wouldn't have been out of character.

And now, if she got to Chad before I did, Chad, to borrow a phrase from one of our distinguished former presidents, was going to be in deep doo-doo.

I was afraid that even Bob Lattner was on his way to Houston. He was obviously mixed up in things, though just how wasn't clear to me. As I drove along at fifteen miles an hour over the speed limit, I tried to think of all the different ways the pieces could be moved around and made to fit together.

Everything would have been much simpler if people had just told me all they knew right from the beginning, but no one ever wants to do that, not even Dino, who was supposed to be my friend.

OK, he *was* my friend. But he'd withheld information that might have helped me. It might have helped Patrick Mullen, who was probably dead by now if I was right about Chad.

It might have helped Henry J., too, not that I was going to spend a lot of time mourning his loss.

I wouldn't mourn Chad Peavy for very long, either, but I didn't want Big Al or Bob Lattner to get to him before I did. I wanted him punished, but not the way they'd go about it.

WHEN I TURNED onto Coleridge, I saw that I wasn't the first to arrive. There was a big black Cadillac parked at the curb near the Peavy house. The night was quiet, however, and there were only a few lights on in the neighboring homes. It clearly wasn't a war zone, not yet at any rate. Maybe the Cadillac belonged to someone who lived nearby.

Right. And maybe there was no saltwater in the Gulf of Mexico.

I parked the truck about a block from the Peavy house and got out. The sky hadn't gotten any less cloudy, but in Houston there were plenty of streetlights. As I approached the Caddy, I thought I could see the bulky outline of someone sitting in the driver's seat.

When I got to the car, I bent down to look inside. Big Al stared back at me. I signed for her to roll down the window. She switched on the key, pushed a button, and the window slid down.

"What're you doing here, Smith?" she asked.

"Shopping for a house. I thought a move to the city might give me a different perspective on things."

"Henry J. told me once that you used to be a football player. A pretty good one."

"I played football. I'm not sure how good I was. What's that got to do with anything?"

"I was wondering if all football players were smart-asses or if it was just you."

"All of them, pretty much," I said. "There's something I've been wondering about, too."

"What?"

"What are *you* doing here?"

"I think you know the answer to that one. I'm going to feed the kid who lives in there to the crabs."

"Are you going to tell me why?"

"You know that one, too. He killed Henry J."

"I know that, but I don't know why."

"There's a lot of things you don't know, Smith. You're not nearly as smart as you think you are."

"Why don't you help me out, then? Tell me what's going on."

"You'll find out soon enough," she said, bringing her hand up from her lap.

There was a snub-barreled Colt Python in her fist, and it was pointed at my head. Some women would have found the .357 Magnum uncomfortably large. Not Big Al.

"Back away a little," she said. "Keep your hands where I can see them."

I did what she said. Just thinking about what a .357 bullet could do to my head was enough to make me very careful.

Big Al opened the door of the car and got out.

"I was wondering how I was going to get in the house," she said. "I'm glad you came along. The Peavys know you."

"What if I won't help you?"

"You will," she said, waggling the Colt, and of course I did.

MR. PEAVY DIDN'T look nearly as happy to see me as he had the last time I'd paid him a visit.

"What are you doing here at this hour?" he asked, looking at me through a crack between the door and the facing. "Is this about getting Chad back in school?"

It was about something a lot more unpleasant than that, but I couldn't say so because Big Al was standing behind me, ready to blow a hole the size of a softball in me.

"It's urgent that I talk to Chad," I said, which was certainly true.

"You don't look so good," he said. "What happened?"

I hadn't had a chance to clean up much in the last few hours, so

I'm sure I didn't look at all like someone who was trying to keep kids in school.

"That's what I need to speak to Chad about. Can I come in?"

"Who's that with you?" he asked.

The porch light was on, but Big Al was standing behind me, in my shadow. I'm fairly big, but Big Al is bigger, hence her name, and there was no way she could hide herself completely.

"It's one of the school counselors," I said.

"Well, I don't know," Mr. Peavy said. "This is a pretty strange time to be conducting business, if you ask me."

Big Al stepped out from behind me and pointed the pistol at him.

"Nobody asked you, asshole. Open the damn door."

Mr. Peavy was quicker than I'd have thought, but Big Al could move fast for her size. When Peavy tried to shut the door, she snatched open the screen and kicked the door into his face. While he was still staggering backward, she darted into the room with the Python in a two-handed grip, sweeping it to cover the whole area.

I went in right behind her, and by that time I had my own pistol in hand, hoping I could control the situation before it got out of control.

"Where's the kid?" Big Al asked.

Peavy didn't answer. He was holding his hand to his face where the door had hit him. He was going to have a really bad black eye in the morning.

"Time to forget about the boy," I told Big Al.

She turned around and saw my gun. It didn't seem to bother her much.

She laughed and said, "You think you can stop me with that toy?"

"Yeah," I said. "I do."

"Maybe so," she said, wiggling the Python, "but mine's bigger than yours. It'll take you two or three shots to drop me, and by then, you won't have a spine left."

"You wouldn't want to kill me," I said, wondering how true it was. "So far you've stayed out of jail. You don't want to spoil your record."

"Too late for that," Bob Lattner said as he came through the front door.

35

I HAVE NO idea what Mr. Peavy thought was going on. I wasn't even sure what I thought, except that there were a lot of guns being waved around.

Lattner had a .38 revolver, and for a minute I thought Big Al would play the "mine is bigger than yours" game with him, too. It seemed to give her a lot of satisfaction.

She didn't want to play, however. She said, "You're a little out of your jurisdiction, Lattner. There's nothing you can do about me here."

"We'll see about that. Where's your son, Mr. Peavy?"

Peavy was looking from one pistol to the other as if he'd wandered onto the set of some movie he hadn't even known was being made. He still had one hand up to his face.

"Chad's upstairs," he said. "Asleep."

"No I'm not," Chad said from above us.

He was standing on the landing, and just to make things perfect, he had a pistol, too. Another .38. All we needed now was for his mother to come wandering in with an AK–47 and the evening would be complete.

I've discovered that there's one big problem with having four pistols scattered around a room, even if one of them is yours: You really can't watch all three of the others, not at the same time.

The one I wasn't watching at the moment belonged to Big Al, and naturally she was the first to pull a trigger. The noise was as loud as you would expect an explosion in a living room to be, and it was rapidly followed by another explosion and then another.

The good news was that no one had shot me.

The bad news was that by the time I realized I hadn't been shot, I couldn't have heard the U.S. Marine Band if they'd been playing a Sousa march in the next room.

Everyone was ducking for cover except for Mr. Peavy, who just dropped to the floor and assumed the fetal position.

Big Al was behind the sofa, while Lattner and I had opted for chairs.

Chad fired a couple of shots at the room in general and dashed back upstairs.

That still left three of us armed and dangerous, but none of us was willing to make the first move to come out from behind the furniture.

It seemed to me that someone had to do something eventually, but I hated to be the one. Shooting at people bothers me. I don't like the results.

On the other hand, if someone had to get shot, I'd prefer that it not be me, so I rolled out from behind the chair, fired a shot under the sofa, and hit Big Al in the foot.

She didn't make much noise, no more than a mild groan, or that's what it sounded like to me. Maybe she screamed in agony. I couldn't really hear, so I wouldn't know for sure. Say what you will about her, though, she was tough.

So was Lattner, who'd apparently been hit by Chad's first shot. There was a dark stain spreading on the back of his jacket, but with Big Al out of the picture for the time being he took the opportunity to charge across the room to the stairs.

Sometimes people can fool you. I would have said that Mr. Peavy wouldn't move for about a week.

I would have been wrong.

He rolled in front of Lattner, who tripped over him and fell forward, striking his head on the first step of the stairway. His pistol flew out of his hand and landed four steps up.

I headed for the stairway. Big Al was still behind the couch, and Lattner wasn't moving. If anyone was going to catch up with Chad, it was going to be me. Mr. Peavy tried to trip me the way he'd gotten

Lattner, but I was too quick for him and dodged out of the way. Having seen him in action, I was ready for him.

I stooped down and grabbed Lattner's pistol on my way up the stairs. You never knew when a spare might come in handy in a crowd like the one I was fooling with.

I reached the second floor and looked down the hallway. Mrs. Peavy was standing outside her bedroom door in a green nightgown, staring at me. She wasn't holding an AK–47, thank goodness. Not even a .38.

"What's happening?" she said. "Where's my husband?"

I was sure she was talking loudly, but I could barely hear her. My ears were still ringing from the gunshots.

"He's downstairs," I said. My voice seemed to echo in my skull. "He's fine, but some others aren't. It might be a good idea to call 911. Where's Chad?"

She looked at the pistols in my hands, then at a door at the end of the hall.

"I don't know," she said.

I left her there and ran to the door. It was locked. With the shape my knee was in, I wasn't going to be kicking it open. I stood to the side and shot the lock to pieces.

I went into the room carefully, but the care wasn't necessary. Chad wasn't there. The window opposite the door was open, and there was a big sycamore tree just outside.

I was in no condition for tree-climbing. I went back downstairs, where Lattner was lying where he'd fallen. Big Al, on the other hand, was standing up and pointing the Colt at me. I was getting tired of looking at it, so I shot her again, in the arm this time. She fell back behind the couch.

Mr. Peavy was sitting on the floor, looking at me with wild eyes. He was no doubt reconsidering having his son enroll in any college or university that would hire a two-gun maniac like me.

I handed him Lattner's pistol. "If either of them tries anything, pull the trigger," I said, and ran outside.

There were plenty of lights on in most of the surrounding houses now. Mrs. Peavy might be calling 911, but so were half the neighbors. The cops would be on the way before she said ten words.

Chad was running down the sidewalk. He had half a block's head start on me, but I started after him anyway. I was in pretty decent shape, thanks to my almost daily run, and although he was a football player and much younger than I was, I didn't think he'd been working out lately.

The problem was my knee. I was afraid it wouldn't hold up long enough for me to catch him.

I suppose I could have fired a few shots at him, but the truth is that a pistol is rarely accurate at any distance beyond thirty yards, and I was already breathing heavily, which is not conducive to unerring aim. In other words, I was as likely to hit a nearby house as to hit Chad. More likely, in fact. Even if I thought I could hit him, I couldn't be certain that I wouldn't kill him. And I didn't want to do that. Not even if he was a murderer.

So I pounded along behind him, wishing that I was twenty years younger and a few pounds lighter. Having a sound knee would've been nice, too.

But you have to make do with what you have, which in my case was an aging body and a knee that was already beginning to cause me to list alarmingly to one side.

We ran for two blocks, and I thought I might actually be gaining, but if I was, the gain was so small that it was measurable in millimeters.

Chad wasn't pulling away, however; I was sure of that. That was the good news.

The bad news was that my knee felt as if something inside it might be about to fly apart. I wasn't going to be able to go much farther.

Luckily, I didn't have to. Chad fell down.

It was an old neighborhood, and some of the trees near the sidewalk had sent their roots under it, cracking the concrete and making it dangerously uneven. I had barely missed stubbing my toe a couple of times, and when Chad went down I wasn't terribly surprised.

The surprise came when he twisted around and shot me.

I hadn't thought he'd do it, though I should have known better. He'd shot at Sharon, killed Henry J., and had most likely eliminated Patrick Mullen as well.

Why shouldn't he shoot me, too?

My leg went out from under me as if jerked by a rope. I fell on my shoulder and rolled into the street. The curb wasn't very high, but it was better than no cover at all.

Chad's next bullet chipped concrete a foot from my head and screamed away. The one after that came a little closer, but not much. It did, however, hit something: a car across the street. That's what I mean by accuracy being affected by exertion. He was lucky to have hit my leg. Or I was unlucky. One or the other.

I tried to slow my breathing, and I gripped the Mauser with both hands.

"Chad," I said. "Put down the pistol. The police are on the way, and I don't want to have to shoot you."

That was true. I really didn't want to shoot him, but he said, "Fuck you," so I did.

36

"YOU TWO MAKE quite a pair," Cathy Macklin said.

I suppose she was right. Dino was still wearing his sling, though I don't think he really needed it. He was using the old sympathy ploy with Evelyn, so she wouldn't pay too much attention to me. He thought I was getting entirely too much attention from Cathy, and for Evelyn to feel sorry for me too was more than he could take.

I was playing the injured hero part to the hilt, limping around like a buzzard with a broken talon. I'd had more stitches than Dino, so I felt I had to seem more wounded. It wasn't exactly the macho approach, but it seemed to be working. So I smiled at Cathy's remark.

"She didn't mean that in a good way," Evelyn said, seeing my face. "She meant that you two are crazy. You should be ashamed of yourself, Tru, shooting a helpless young man like that. And you—" she looked at Dino "—you should get a real job and stay out of trouble."

We were at Dino's house, but for a wonder the TV wasn't on and we were able to talk without having to shout over the rantings of the exercise guy. I was drinking a Big Red straight from the bottle. Dino was having a little Wild Turkey and water, while Cathy and Evelyn were drinking some kind of white wine. Evelyn had brought it. Dino doesn't keep white wine in the house. He thinks it's even worse than Big Red.

There was a small artificial Christmas tree in one corner of the room. Dino hadn't set it up, of course; Evelyn had. It was even decorated with lights and balls, and there were a few presents under it. I'd snooped around it a little, being a detective, after all, and there was one with my name on it. I had no idea what it could be, although I'd shaken it a time or two.

"I was thinking about asking Dino to go to work for me," I told Evelyn. "But I'm not sure I could trust him."

Dino looked hurt. "When have I ever lied to you?" he asked.

I didn't even bother to answer.

"I helped you crack the Kirbo case, didn't I?" he asked.

"Hindered me is more like it. If you'd told me about Sharon sooner, you might have saved me some trouble. Her, too. I would have been a lot more careful with Chad Peavy."

I wasn't absolutely sure that was the truth, but it sounded like the right thing to say. If there was any irony in the situation, I didn't see it.

"The one you should have been careful with was that cop, Lattner," Dino said. "I always told you that you shouldn't go to the cops."

In that case, he'd been right. And calling the cops had been someone else's mistake, too. Henry J.'s. Along with Dino and Big Al, he was the last person in the world I would have expected to call the police, but that's what he'd done. He thought he had a good reason, however.

On the night of the party it had been Chad, not Randall, who'd slipped the GHB into Kelly Davis's drink. Randall had been too drunk to do much of anything and hadn't even known what was going on. Kelly had had a bad reaction to the GHB, and after only about an hour had slipped into a coma. Then she'd stopped breathing altogether.

Chad had panicked and told Henry J., who was there to provide whatever the kids needed for a good time—liquor, drugs, and probably even barbecued ribs if anyone had asked for them—as long as someone could pay.

Henry J. had called Lattner, who was Big Al's tame cop. He was the one who'd called her at the Hurricane Club and tried to blame me and Dino for Henry J.'s death. That was why the call had arrived so late; Lattner hadn't been able to get to a safe phone to make it.

When Lattner arrived at the party, Henry J. had sent everyone away except for Chad and Randall. When Lattner found out that the dead girl was his own niece, who had actually spoken with him on the phone that very afternoon, he went berserk.

Chad blamed Randall for everything, Henry J. went along with him, and Randall was too out of it to defend himself. Lattner had begun hitting him. Randall fell down, and Lattner kicked him in the head. The kick was probably what killed him, but we'd never know for sure. His body was somewhere in the Gulf, and unlike Kelly Davis's, it hadn't washed up where it could be found.

Henry J. had called Big Al, who had come to the house with a friend who had a boat. The two of them took care of the bodies, though not very well. Apparently they hadn't weighted Kelly Davis's carefully. We'd never know for sure, since Big Al claimed that she hadn't been involved, and the friend was currently sailing somewhere on the blue waters off the coast of Mexico. Or so Big Al said. I had a feeling he wouldn't be showing up in Galveston again, no matter where he was.

While the bodies were being taken care of, Chad started working on a story about what had happened to Randall. He and Henry J. had originally planned some story about how Randall and the Davis girl had met at the party and run away together, but the sudden reappearance of her body had ruined that one. So Chad just told everyone that Randall had disappeared.

Lattner had gotten himself assigned to the Kirbo case so he could keep things covered up, and he'd been pretty successful. The only other kid that Chad had met at the party was Patrick Mullen, and Lattner had talked to him to make sure he didn't know enough to hurt anyone. He'd also assured him that there was no need for him to worry about things, that the investigation was going just fine.

When I started poking into things, everyone got worried, but Chad was the one who'd panicked. Again. He wasn't a professional like the others, and he'd decided that he'd eliminate the witnesses.

He and his father had taken a handgun class together, and they were both licensed to carry. So Chad was thoroughly familiar with his .38. He'd tried for Sharon, taken out Henry J., and missed on Patrick Mullen, who'd been visiting his grandmother in Pasadena. He was a lucky guy, that time at least.

When it dawned on Lattner that Dino and I hadn't killed Henry J., he realized that Chad was on a rampage, and went after him.

So had Big Al, of course. Chad should have thought about the consequences of his actions, but if he'd been the kind to do that, he never would have tried using GHB in the first place.

"How's the cop doing, by the way?" Dino asked.

"He'll be all right," I said. "He lost a lot of blood, but they patched him up. Anyway, he's not a cop anymore."

"Yeah, they don't like to keep guys like him on the force," Dino said. "Sets a bad example. But he's no worse than the rest of them."

I was never going to convince Dino that there were a lot of good law enforcement officers, so I didn't even try. Old prejudices die hard.

"What about the boy?" Cathy asked.

"He's OK," I said. "If he'd had a little more fat on him, he'd be even better. And he wasn't defenseless. He shot me first."

Even though Chad had been trying to kill me, I'd tried to shoot him in the side, avoiding any major organs. He was so lean that there hadn't been much loose skin for the bullet to pass through, and I'd broken one of his ribs. That was the least of his problems, however. He wouldn't be enrolling at Texas Tech again for a long, long time.

"I feel sorry for the Kirbos," Evelyn said. "They seemed like such nice people."

I felt sorry for them, too, especially Janey, who I was afraid was going to have real problems with Tack. He blamed himself for what had happened, and from what Dino had told me, he hadn't reformed. In fact, when they'd returned home, his drinking had gotten suddenly much worse. He hadn't been sober for more than five minutes since we'd told them about Randall. Evelyn had gone with us to talk to them at the Galvez after we found out the truth, since Dino thought having her along might help Janey. I wasn't sure that it had.

"Did you mean what you said about us working together?" Dino asked me.

"We wouldn't be able to get along. You have to be able to trust your partner."

"I trust you. And you can trust me, too. I promise."

He smiled toothily and made an attempt to look trustworthy, which was sort of like a panther trying to look like a vegetarian.

"The kind of work I do is mostly pretty boring," I said. "It involves sitting in front of a computer all day."

"That couldn't be much worse than sitting in front of the home shopping channel all day," Evelyn said.

"Hey, I don't just sit." Dino indicated some of his workout equipment. "I get a lot of exercise. I'd miss that."

"You'd get plenty of exercise on some of the things Tru works on," Cathy told him. "I wish he'd spend more time in front of the computer and a lot less on these jobs you bring him."

I wished it, too. Dino's jobs never seemed to end the way they should. Too many people got hurt. The Peavys, whose son would be in prison. The Kirbos, who would never see their son again.

I'd gotten a call from Kelly Davis's mother, though, to thank me. There's always some good even in the worst things, I suppose.

And then there was Big Al, who'd gotten off again. There was no proof that she'd ever been directly involved in the deaths of Kelly or Randall, or even that she'd aided in the disposal of the bodies. She'd forced her way into the Peavy home, and she'd fired her pistol there, but those were minor things. And she had a very good lawyer.

I drank the last of my Big Red and set the bottle down on Dino's coffee table.

"I have an idea," I said. "Why don't we all go out to eat tonight?"

"Who's buying?" Dino asked.

"My treat," I said.

"Where will we go?" Cathy asked.

"I'd like some Mexican food," I said. "How does that sound?"

"It sounds good to me," Evelyn said.

"All right," I said, getting to my feet. "I know this place where they have great enchiladas."

I had limped almost to the door before Dino started yelling.

Afterword

WHEN I WAS a child, I thought Galveston Island was one of the most romantic places in Texas. Many years later, I still think so, and writing a series of novels about Truman Smith, who's fortunate enough to live there, has been a tremendous pleasure for me. If you've ever visited Galveston, you can surely understand a bit about the fascination the place has for nearly everyone. If you haven't visited there but you'd like to, you can take a virtual trip any time at all by visiting the city's Web site at http://www.galvestontourism.com. It's a trip you won't regret.